THE TWO JULIANNES

When Julianne was in the gentle and considerate company of her husband-to-be, Lord William Rutherford, she felt deliciously protected from all harm and as fully in command of both her good sense and her senses as any proper young lady could be.

But when Julianne was alone with the cynical and mocking John Champernoun, she was assaulted by emotions that could properly be regarded only as infamous, as she felt herself rebelling against the role she was born to play as an aristocratic young beauty and a future member of one of England's ruling families.

One man clearly brought out the best in her. The other, most certainly the worst.

If only she could be sure which was which. . . .

Lord Richard's Daughter

SIGNET Regency Romances You'll Enjoy

Lord Richard's Daughter

by
Joan Wolf

Ⓢ
A SIGNET BOOK
NEW AMERICAN LIBRARY
TIMES MIRROR

NAL BOOKS ARE AVAILABLE AT QUANTITY DISCOUNTS
WHEN USED TO PROMOTE PRODUCTS OR SERVICES. FOR
INFORMATION PLEASE WRITE TO PREMIUM MARKETING
DIVISION, THE NEW AMERICAN LIBRARY, INC.,
1633 BROADWAY, NEW YORK, NEW YORK 10019.

SIGNET TRADEMARK REG. U.S. PAT. OFF. AND FOREIGN COUNTRIES
REGISTERED TRADEMARK—MARCA REGISTRADA
HECHO EN CHICAGO, U.S.A.

SIGNET, SIGNET CLASSICS, MENTOR, PLUME,
MERIDIAN AND NAL BOOKS
are published by The New American Library, Inc.,
1633 Broadway, New York, New York 10019

First Printing, July, 1983

1 2 3 4 5 6 7 8 9

PRINTED IN THE UNITED STATES OF AMERICA

Chapter One

December 1814

To leve my frinds, my fortune, my attempte,
To leve the purpose I so longe had sought
And holde both cares, and cumforts in contempt.
　　　　　—Sir Walter Ralegh

The Dowager Duchess of Crewe stood in the doorway of her drawing room and contemplated the man who had requested an interview with her. She had recognized his family name immediately: it was one of the most ancient in England. But she did not recall ever having met this particular Champernoun before.

He was standing with his back to her, apparently absorbed in a portrait that was hanging on the far wall. He looked to be extraordinarily tall. "Mr. Champernoun?" she inquired, a trifle imperiously.

The man turned and she knew at once she had never seen him before. One would not forget that face. He was dressed correctly, in buff pantaloons and blue superfine coat, but somehow he did not look quite civilized. His straight, ebony-colored hair was a trifle too long. He smiled, showing very white teeth, and crossed the room, greeting her in a voice that was deep, educated, and indefinably loaded with authority.

The beautiful old woman nodded graciously in response. "I do not believe we have met," she said pleasantly, "but of course I know your name. Are you related to the Earl of Denham?"

"He is my cousin."

"I see." She smiled at him. "What may I do for you, Mr. Champernoun?".

"I have brought you something, Your Grace. From Egypt." He was speaking slowly, almost carefully.

"Ah," said the duchess, comprehension dawning. "Egypt." She thought he might almost have passed for an Egyptian himself, with that black hair and those straight black brows. But his height gave him away. And his eyes. Meeting them full, the duchess felt a little shock of surprise. One did not expect to find such a brilliant blue green looking out of that deeply sunburned face. She couldn't quite read their expression; it might almost have been pity. "Have you brought me news of my son?" she asked sharply.

"I have brought you your granddaughter," he answered.

"Julianne?" the old woman said on a note of fear. "What is Julianne doing in England?"

"I brought her with me on my ship. I am in England on a mission for the pasha."

"Is my son dead?" The duchess's voice sounded harsh in her own ears.

"Yes, Your Grace," came the grave reply. "I am sorry to have to tell you that he is." She felt a strong hand under her arm and in a minute she was sitting on the sofa. "Let me procure you a glass of wine," he was saying. She shook her head but he did not seem to notice. The butler came into the room and in a short time a glass of Madeira was in her hand. "Drink it," said a calm voice and she did.

She put the glass down. "I am all right now." She spoke with dignity. "It was the shock." She turned and looked at the man who was sitting now in a chair close by. After a moment she asked collectedly, "What happened to Richard, Mr. Champernoun? Was it the natives or the fever?"

There was an almost imperceptible pause before he replied. "The fever, Your Grace. He was in a very primitive part of Abyssinia when he became ill. I believe he did not suffer long."

"I see."

"Your granddaughter will be able to tell you more details. She was with him at the time."

The dowager duchess rose to her feet. "You were looking at his picture when I came in, Mr. Champernoun." She walked across the room to stand before it herself.

He followed her. "I wondered if it were Lord Richard. I did not know him myself."

The two of them stood for a moment in silence, regarding the portrait before them. It was of a young man dressed in a black coat and holding a book in his hands. However, it was not the pose but the face that riveted the eye. John Champernoun thought that he had never seen modern features that so closely resembled the ideal of classic Greek beauty. "Is it like him?" he asked.

"It doesn't do him justice," his mother replied. "Next to Richard, Apollo would have looked second-rate. And what good did his looks ever do him? He went into the Church, a perfectly appropriate profession for a second son, but was he satisfied with the excellent living he had here at Crewe? No. Richard could never be satisfied with a normal life. He had to have a cause."

Champernoun looked from the duchess's face back to the pictured face of her son. Lord Richard was indeed beautiful, but Champernoun was not surprised at the character his mother gave him. That stern young face did not look gentle or yielding. There was something implacable in the line of the straight classic nose, in the Athenian purity of mouth and chin and brow. He himself knew something of Lord Richard from his daughter and he was curious to see if Richard's mother's assessment would be similar. "However did the son of a duke come to be a missionary in Africa?" he asked.

The duchess's mouth tightened. "He began as an active member of the antislavery movement;

that was where he met Mr. Wilberforce and his friends. Richard was one of the founding members of the Church Missionary Society for Africa and the East. The idea was to concentrate anti-slavery efforts on Africa, where the traffic was most extensive. But they could get no one to go out to East Africa. Richard wanted to go. We fought with him for years and finally, in 1809, we could hold him no longer. He went and with him he took Judith, his wife, and Julianne, who was fourteen at the time."

"East Africa is hard on women and children," Champernoun said noncommittally.

"I begged him to leave Julianne with me, but he would not listen. The comforts and amenities of life had no meaning for Richard. His soul was always straining after higher things. He could not rest, and he did not approve of others' resting either. Certainly not his wife or daughter. Judith died after only a year."

There was silence in the room for a full minute, then the duchess turned to John Champernoun. "I was very angry with Richard, but I learned to forgive him. He could not help what he was. He was, I suppose, a great man. But he was not a comfortable man. He was not a good son or husband or father. Poor Julianne. What a life she must have led!"

There was suddenly an expression on the lean, dark face before her that caught the duchess's attention. "I believe Miss Wells is something of a strong character herself," he said.

"She always adored her father," sighed the

duchess. Then, giving herself a visible mental shake, she turned to the present. "How did you come to be my granddaughter's escort, Mr. Champernoun? You said you did not know my son."

"No, Your Grace, I did not. Lord Richard, as you know, was charged with creating a series of twelve mission stations along the banks of the Nile from Alexandria to Abyssinia. He was not far from Harar when he became ill and died. He left your granddaughter completely unprotected. She managed to get to Harar, and fortunately I happened to be in the city—in disguise, of course. As I said, it was fortunate I was there. A blond unveiled girl walking on the streets of a Moslem city does not go unnoticed. Harar, besides being a sacred city, is also a center of the slave trade. Fair-haired women are deeply prized in Africa."

"Oh my God." The duchess looked horrified.

"She is all right, but she had a very unpleasant experience, Your Grace. I brought her back to Cairo with me, and then when Mohammed Ali— the Egyptian Pasha—asked me to undertake a mission to London as his representative, it seemed the perfect opportunity to bring Miss Wells home."

"Do you mean Julianne has been in your company, unchaperoned, for all this time?" The duchess looked even more horrified than she had at the suggestion of the slave market.

Champernoun regarded her with amusement. "She has been perfectly safe, Your Grace. I managed to control my animal instincts."

"So you say," the old lady returned tartly. "It

is what everyone else will say that concerns me."

"There is no reason for anyone at all to know that Julianne has been in my company. As I told you, I was in disguise when I was in Harar. No Christian may enter a Moslem holy city, you understand. And no one in Cairo knew of her presence. The crew of my ship will not talk." He smiled at the duchess with calculated charm. "I suggest you say that your granddaughter was escorted to France by a Frenchwoman to whose care she was commended by Lord Richard. There are plenty of French in Egypt now. And, if you can procure some respectable woman for me quickly, I will escort both Miss Wells and chaperon here tomorrow. We will announce we have come from France."

The duchess looked at him doubtfully and his eyes suddenly narrowed. "If you want me to marry your granddaughter, I will," he drawled, a note of contempt in his deep voice. "But like Lord Richard, I am not the material out of which good husbands are made. I like my freedom too much. Miss Wells can do much better."

"I am sure she can," said the duchess, stung by the note in his voice. "Very well, Mr. Champernoun, I will go along with your arrangements. I am quite sure Julianne's former nurse will be willing to act as chaperon. She lives in a cottage on the grounds of Crewe. Where is Julianne staying?"

"At the King's Inn, Harwich."

"Mrs. Brightling will be there by evening."

There was a gleam of what could have been mockery in those sea-blue eyes, but his voice was perfectly courteous as he answered, "Yes, Your Grace," and took his departure.

Chapter Two

My hopes cleane out of sight, with forced wind
To kyngdomes strange, to lands farr off addrest.
—Sir Walter Ralegh

Julianne arrived at the Dower House of Crewe
the following day accompanied by Mrs. Brightling,
her old nurse, and by John Champernoun. Mr.
Champernoun did not stay long and the duchess
watched closely as he made his farewells to her
granddaughter. The two of them were very composed and quite properly formal. Nothing in their
outward appearance did anything to contradict
the story Champernoun had told her the previous day. But there was something there, something
unspoken and subterranean, that the old woman
sensed in the air between the beautiful fair-haired
girl who was her granddaughter and the tall,
dark, and unnervingly masculine man who had
been Julianne's escort.

After Champernoun had left, the duchess
turned to her granddaughter with gentle concern.

"Are you all right, my love? You have had a terrible experience, I fear."

There was an odd, almost blind look in Julianne's eyes and it took a moment before they appeared to focus on her grandmother. "I beg your pardon, Grandmama?" she said faintly.

"Julianne, was Mr. Champernoun—ah, did he treat you respectfully? He didn't hurt you in any way, did he?"

Julianne's wide darkly lashed eyes were now steady on her grandmother's face. "No, he did not hurt me," she said very calmly. The faintest of smiles quirked the corner of her mouth. "I can't say he treated me respectfully, however. That would be doing it a bit too brown. I doubt if Mr. Champernoun treats *anyone* respectfully, Grandmama."

"Yes, I can believe that," the dowager duchess said with comical exasperation.

Julianne laughed. "Mr. Champernoun is rather a law unto himself, I'm afraid. Papa once called him a renegade and I suppose he is. He is also a mercenary. But he was very kind to me. I shudder to think what would have become of me but for him."

The dowager duchess looked very bleak. "Your father is greatly to blame, my dear. It was bad enough to tear you away from your home, your friends, your country—but then to go and die leaving you totally unprotected in the middle of Africa! No other man but Richard would have done such a thing."

"He did not mean to die," said Julianne wearily.

"And you knew Papa, Grandmama. He never even thought of such a thing happening. He never thought of the things that concern other people."

"I know that all too well," snapped Lord Richard's mother. There was a moment's silence, then the dowager duchess's features relaxed and she smiled at Julianne. "Well, you are with me now, my love. Safe. And I mean to take very good care of you."

"Thank you, Grandmama. It is good to be here."

"Would you like some refreshment or shall I show you to your room?"

A glimmer appeared in Julianne's strangely luminous eyes. "Do you know what I would like more than anything in the world, Grandmama?"

"What is that, my love?"

"A bath!"

The dowager duchess laughed and began to walk toward the stairs. "Then a bath you shall have. Come along and I'll show you to your room."

The steaming tub in front of the fireplace looked marvelous to Julianne's deprived eyes. Impatiently she allowed her grandmother's maid to undress her, anxious to submerge herself in the hot soapy water. It took the maid's startled exclamation as she drew Julianne's dress off her shoulders to divert her attention from the pleasures of the tub. "Oh, Miss Wells!" the maid cried. "Whatever happened to your shoulders?"

Julianne knew what was there even before she looked; she had seen the marks this morning. In the excitement of her homecoming she had forgotten them, but now as she looked slowly down at her upper arms she saw that they had not faded during the course of the day.

Julianne had extremely delicate skin, fair and close-textured like a baby's. The dark ugly bruises were very clear against its white silkiness. The bruises showed, to Julianne's uneasy eyes, the unmistakable outlines of a man's hard fingers. She looked up to find the maid's horrified gaze still on her shoulders. "It's all right. I almost had an accident and one of the sailors grabbed me. He saved me from a nasty fall, but I was left with this legacy." She was relieved to hear that her voice sounded normal; her heart, however, was hammering.

"He must have been very strong, miss, to have done that," said the maid.

"Yes," said Julianne. There was very faint color in her cheeks. "He was."

After her bath she dressed in her blue merino dress again and was sitting having her hair done when the dowager duchess came back into the room.

"Don't you have another dress to change into, Julianne?" her grandmother asked. "That one, I regret to tell you, is sadly unfashionable."

"Is it?" responded Julianne composedly. "I rather like it. John bought it for me in Harwich and I am afraid it is the only one I own."

The duchess's ear registered that "John" immediately. "What were you wearing before you entered Harwich?" she asked suspiciously.

Julianne grinned. "Turkish trousers."

"Trousers!"

"Yes. And they are most amazingly comfortable. I assure you I parted from them with a pang."

"Trousers," said the dowager duchess again, this time with loathing. Julianne chuckled. "Tomorrow, my dear, we will see about getting you some clothes," the dowager duchess went on, ignoring Julianne's unseemly mirth. "I do not think you need to wear mourning; Richard has been dead for almost half a year. No. Some lavenders, perhaps. And white." She tilted her head and looked appraisingly at her granddaughter. Julianne's hair was darker than her father's, more a honey than a silver blond, but it was thick and shining and dressed now in a stylish mode by Parker, the dowager duchess's abigail, it looked beautiful. She did not have her father's celestial blue eyes. Julianne's were of a cool shining gray, peculiarly luminous, widely spaced, and large, with surprisingly dark lashes and brows. She was tall, with a long slender neck and magnolia fair skin.

"You have the Wells looks," the dowager duchess said to her with pardonable pride. "That is at least one good thing that Richard did for you."

"Papa did a number of good things for me, Grandmama," said Julianne quietly. "We both of us have got to try to remember that."

Her grandmother took her shopping for clothes and took her up to Crewe to meet her uncle the duke, his wife, and his children. One of her cousins, Caroline, was a year younger than Julianne and the two girls were thrown together a great deal that winter. For the first time in her life Julianne led the life that a girl of her age and class and family would normally lead in the English society of her day. She and her cousin were to be presented to society in the spring and a great deal of their time was spent preparing for this great event.

Julianne was grimly determined to forget the past and throw herself into the future her grandmother was planning for her. The most immediate goal of the dowager duchess's campaign was to find her granddaughter a husband, and this was a plan Julianne was not at all averse to. It seemed to her that a husband and home of her own were what she most wanted in the world. She was tired of wandering, tired of rootlessness, tired of always being a stranger. John had once said to her, "Home is wherever night finds me." But that wasn't good enough for her. She wanted security. And she wanted a man who could give her the security she craved—a man who would in no way resemble John Champernoun.

Julianne spent a remarkable amount of time that winter trying not to think about John Champernoun. She visited her aunt, rode with Caroline, and went to the shops with her grandmother. She revised and reorganized the diary she had kept during her years in Africa. And she entered with determined enthusiasm into all her grandmother's plans for her coming London season.

The event that launched Julianne into London

society was a ball which was given jointly by the dowager duchess and the present Duchess of Crewe in honor of Julianne and her cousin Caroline. It was a very lavish affair, attended by all the right people, and was pronounced by so eminent a critic as Lady Jersey to be a great success. Julianne was a great success as well. She wore a gown of pale blue crepe over a white satin slip and looked, her grandmother thought mistily, rather like a lily. Certainly the dozens of young men to whom she was introduced regarded her with blatant admiration.

None of the young men made a reciprocal impression upon Julianne, however. In fact, out of the entire evening there was only one person who stood out in her memory.

She was sitting on one of the gilt chairs surrounding the dance floor waiting for one of the ubiquitous young men to bring her a glass of punch when an older man than the boys she had danced with all evening came over and sat beside her. "Miss Wells, I'm Robert Southland," he said. "Your aunt introduced me earlier."

"Oh, yes," she replied vaguely. Her Aunt Elizabeth had introduced a host of men to her this evening. She smiled politely and said, "Are you enjoying yourself, Mr. Southland?"

The man shrugged. "They're all the same, these crushes."

Julianne laughed. "Oh dear. That isn't a very encouraging thing to say to a girl whose fate it is to attend them all."

He grinned at her. He had an open good-natured

face with bright brown eyes. "I understand you and your father spent a good deal of time in Egypt," he said.

"Yes," she responded cautiously. "We were there."

"You didn't by any chance meet a man called John Champernoun?" he asked.

At the mention of that name Julianne felt her heart turn over. "Why, yes," she answered faintly. "I met him—briefly."

"I understand he's become quite a fixture with the pasha," Southland said. "We were together on the *Tigre* in 1799, you know. I was there when John pulled Mohammed Ali out of the sea. He was one of the Albanians who had come to Egypt with the Turkish expedition against Napoleon. Bonaparte routed them at Aboukir. The sea was filled with fugitives swimming for their lives and John fished out Mohammed Ali. They became good friends after that." He shook his head in wonderment. "Whoever would have thought that that half-drowned fugitive was destined to become the future Pasha of Egypt."

"I doubt if destiny had much to do with it," Julianne said dryly.

He grinned. "Not destiny, eh, but John. You know, it's a damn good thing he chose to stay in Egypt. If he had come home he would certainly have been hanged by now. Goes his own way, does John. Makes his own laws. Best natural fighter I ever saw. I often thought Wellington would have given half his staff in exchange for John if he'd ever seen him in action. I still don't know why he wasn't in the army. Seems the natural place for a man of his talents."

"I doubt if he could stand the discipline of the army," said Julianne, betraying a deeper knowledge of their subject than she had originally confessed to. "He's not a man you can push into a mold."

"That is true," agreed Mr. Southland with a reminiscent grin. "I remember him at Acre. Christ!"

There was a pause. "I did not know John had been at Acre," said Julianne.

Mr. Southland shot her a suddenly shrewd look. "He certainly was. I should go so far as to say he was a good deal responsible for our success." Acre was one of the most famous sieges of the late war; a small contingent of Turks led by Sir Sidney Smith's crew of the *Tigre* had held out for almost two months against the entire French army and had handed Napoleon his first defeat.

Both Julianne and Mr. Southland had their eyes on the young man who was threading his way around the dance floor toward them, two glasses of punch in his hands. "We were both with Sir Sidney Smith until 1803, when the British pulled out of Egypt. I went home, found I had inherited some money, and left the Navy. John stayed in Egypt. He was having too good a time to leave, he told me. Actually, I think he was up to his neck in the power struggle that ended up with Mohammed Ali being named pasha. I remember not being very surprised when it finally happened."

"No," murmured Julianne. "One wouldn't be, I suppose."

The young man had reached them by now and she smiled, accepted the punch, introduced the two men, and after a few minutes Mr. Southland excused himself and went off to the card room.

Julianne obediently got into bed in the early morning after her maid had undressed her and put away her gown. The dowager duchess had been very pleased with the success of both her ball and her granddaughter. "Emily Cowper promised to send around vouchers for Almacks," she told Julianne. "And Mrs. Drummond Burrell complimented me on your looks and behavior—and *she* is very difficult to satisfy, my love. I am very pleased with you. Young Lord Rutherford seemed very taken, I thought."

Julianne smiled absently. "He was very nice, Grandmama."

The old woman looked at her for a minute. "He is the oldest son of the Earl of Minton, one of the greatest men in the country."

"He was very nice," Julianne repeated.

The duchess yawned. "I am tired, my love. I'll bid you good night and seek my bed. You must do the same. I think we will be having visitors tomorrow and I want you to be looking your best."

Julianne kissed her grandmother's soft, scented cheek and walked with her up the stairs to their bedrooms. But after her maid had left the room, Julianne got out of bed, put on a warm robe, and went to sit by the fire.

John. For months now she had been trying not to think of him. But she had only to hear his name mentioned tonight and so much of what she was trying to forget had come rushing back. She closed her eyes and his face was vividly present to her memory: lean, dark, strong, lit by those brilliant, strangely light eyes. So strong was his image that she was vaguely surprised not to find him there when she opened her eyes.

She poked the fire, sat back in her chair, and for the first time since they had parted she allowed herself to think of the things that had happened to her in Africa after the death of her father. She had not told her grandmother the true story, and she had determined that she would forget it herself. But though she had tried, Julianne had not forgotten. She sat now before her comfortable fire and remembered. Remembered the strange and extraordinary circumstances that so many months ago had thrown her into the path of John Champernoun.

Chapter Three

───────◆───────

... captive into Africa.
—Christopher Marlowe

Lord Richard Wells was killed by a lion in Abyssinia. He and his daughter Julianne had been staying with a local king, who upon further acquaintance had proved to be a full-fledged tyrant. Lord Richard had refused to grovel before him as commanded, and Mutesa consequently refused to provide guides and porters so the Wells party could continue on its way. They were detained by the king for five months and one evening Lord Richard wandered out of camp, his Bible his only companion. When she realized he was gone, Julianne took a gun and followed. She heard her father cry out and ran as fast as she could toward the sound. She shot the lion as it was savaging her father's body, but she was too late. Lord Richard's neck was broken. After his death Mutesa sold Julianne to the next Arab slave traders to pass through his territory.

They took her to Harar, a Moslem holy city and center of the slave trade in Abyssinia. Here she was sold again to traders who were taking slaves to Cairo. Julianne was a fair-skinned blonde. The Mamelukes of Egypt prized fair women and were always adding to their harems. She would command a very high price in Egypt. Because she was valuable goods, she was treated well and the trip from Harar to Cairo was not as hellish for her as it was for the unfortunate black slaves who traveled with them. In all her time with the slavers no man attempted to assault her. Virgins commanded more money.

For Julianne the entire experience was a nightmare from which she continually prayed she would awaken. Like her father she had condemned the slave trade, and the traffic in human beings so prevalent in Africa had horrified her. But never had she dreamed that she would be one of the poor unfortunates she had so pitied! It was not possible that she, Julianne Wells, could be sold into some man's harem as if she were chattel. When she got to Cairo she would escape, she told herself, trying to keep her courage up. She would escape and seek sanctuary from one of the Christians who still lived in the city. She thought of the Cairo slave market, of the women she had seen, standing almost naked side by side in pens waiting to be sold, and she shuddered.

She was not sent to the slave market. She was brought to a big house near the Cairo citadel and turned over to a black eunuch. He took her to a very large room where there were gathered a group of other young women, all of whom turned to look at her curiously as she entered. Julianne for her part surveyed them with wonder. There were a number of Circassians as blond as she and several stunning black girls whom she recognized as Ethiopians. The girls had two things in common. They were all dressed in almost transparent shirts and ankle-length Turkish trousers and they were all beautiful.

Julianne was at the house near the citadel for almost a week. During that time she was relentlessly bathed and groomed and painted with cosmetics. She was not going to be sent to the slave market, the other girls told her. She would be offered at a private sale held for the benefit of the powerful Mamelukes, who for centuries had been the real rulers of Egypt.

Julianne knew about the Mamelukes. They were the descendants of Christian slaves who had been brought to Egypt to staff the armies of the sultan. The slaves in turn had become the enslavers and the fighting and intrigue among the Mamelukes had made any kind of organized governmental administration impossible. The Mamelukes had no ties of blood or of interest with the native Egyptians and for centuries had plundered the country for their own aggrandizement. They were still a powerful presence in Egypt, even under the strong-willed Pasha Mohammed Ali. These were the men who would be looking to increase their wealth and prestige by the addition of a blond slave girl to their harems, and so a special

private sale had been arranged for their conven-
ience.

The other girls were pleased and flattered by
what they regarded as the honor of their special
status and they assumed Julianne must feel the
same. Her Arabic was fluent and she made no
attempt to tell her masters or her new compan-
ions that she was English. She remembered vividly the English expedition against Egypt that
had taken place shortly before she and her parents had left for Africa, and she remembered as
well the harsh anti-British sentiments they had
encountered in Cairo when they first arrived.
They had heard stories of how Mohammed Ali,
after defeating the British at Alexandria, had
ridden through Cairo between avenues of British
heads impaled on stakes and of British prisoners
being exhibited in chains before being sold as
slaves. There was still no British embassy in
Cairo to which she could appeal, and Julianne
did not think her nationality would win her any
sympathy from the Arabs into whose hands she
had fallen. They thought she was Circassian and
she left their misconception uncorrected.

The sale took place in the evening in one of the
rooms of the house in which she had been kept
for six days. They did not go out at all into the
teeming, crowded streets of Cairo, where she
might have flung herself out of a carriage and
escaped. The elderly Arab woman who had been
in charge of her regimen throughout the week
made sure she was properly attired for the
occasion. She was dressed in a silk shirt and

Turkish trousers, and the lines of her body were clearly visible through the thin silk fabric. Her lips were artfully reddened and her eyes were outlined with kohl. Her long hair, shining as it had not done in five years, was worn loose to her waist with ribbons laced into it. The other girls were dressed in a similar fashion and then they were brought into a large room where about twenty men reclined on silken cushions.

It was the worst experience of Julianne's life, worse even than the shock of being sold into slavery the first time. She felt the eyes of all those men raking her body, stripping her naked, and she was so outraged and humiliated she thought she would die. She could not look at any of them, but kept her eyes resolutely aloof, fixed on some point in space only she could see. It seemed to go on forever. They were bidding, she realized, and felt hands touch her shoulder, her breast, her hair.

After what seemed to her an eternity it was over and the girls were taken from the room. Julianne, however, did not return with them to her original quarters. "The lord wants you to be taken to his palace immediately, Shajaret ed Durr," the black eunuch told her. Shajaret ed Durr was the name she had been given by the elderly Arab slave mistress. It meant "spray of pearls." They put her into a sedan chair and sent her on her way.

It was dark but the streets of Cairo still streamed with people. Julianne looked out between the curtains of her chair, but what she saw did not reassure her. The people who passed around her chair were ragged and filthy. The dirt of the streets was incredible. And even if she had found the courage to try to make her escape into the twisting alleys and filthy lanes, the two armed men who walked on either side of her chair clearly showed her that escape was impossible.

She was taken to one of the palaces around Lake Ezbekiah. The dam had been cut a month before, and the great lake, filled now with the Nile flood, shimmered in the moonlight. Julianne was firmly escorted from her chair and was surprised to find she was being taken into the main part of the palace and not to the harem. A tall, grave turbaned man took her to a luxurious silk-hung room and left her with the information that "the lord will see you shortly."

Julianne was not easily frightened. She had walked through the ominous silence of the African jungle with scarcely a qualm. She had shot a charging elephant to death as well as the lion that had killed her father. She had clubbed a crocodile and barely escaped an angry hippopotamus, and though her heart had quickened on all those occasions and she had felt fear flicker in her veins, it had not been the paralyzing terror that washed over her now. Out in the jungle she had been a part of nature, and death was all around. The animals killed each other for food. They killed when they, or their young, were threatened. Man too killed when he needed food or when he was threatened. It was all part of the vast, magnificent, beautiful reality of Africa and she had accepted it.

But this was different. There was nothing clean and elemental about this silk-hung room or this low divan heaped with cushions. There was a sound and Julianne looked with fear-darkened eyes toward the door. She would infinitely have preferred to face a lion than the man who stood there on the threshold.

He was very tall, much taller than the ordinary Arab. He wore ankle-length cotton trousers belted by a long sash, a white shirt, and striped vest. On his feet were soft leather slippers that made no sound as he crossed the room toward her. "Greetings, Shajaret ed Durr," he said in Arabic.

"Greetings," Julianne replied breathlessly in the same language. She raised her chin and stiffened her back. No matter what happened she determined he should not see that she was afraid. He stepped a few feet from her and she forced herself to meet his eyes.

She was startled by the brilliant blue-green gaze that looked back at her out of that dark face. Then she remembered—of course, he was a Mameluke, a descendant of Christian slaves; he was not an Arab at all. Courageously she sustained that sea-blue blaze, her own eyes wide with the effort of it. His eyes left hers and thoughtfully looked her up and down. Julianne felt herself go white and then red.

"What nationality are you?" he asked, still speaking in Arabic.

"Circassian," she replied firmly.

He raised a black brow and began to walk toward her again. Before she could prevent herself, she stepped backward. The wall was right behind her; she felt it press against her. He put his hands flat against it, on either side of her, and regarded her closely with narrowed eyes. His face was only inches from hers. "Then I was wrong," he said in the unmistakable accent of Great Britain. "I thought you were English."

Chapter Four

Wherein I spake of most disastrous chances,
Of moving accidents by blood and field;
Of hairbreadth scapes i' th' imminent deadly
breach;
Of being taken by the insolent foe
And sold to slavery . . .

—Shakespeare

The shock of his words caused Julianne's breath to catch audibly in her throat. She stared up at him in astonishment, taking in his lean strongly planed face. He did not look at all English. He looked—dangerous. The blue eyes above her suddenly glinted with comprehension and amusement. "Well?" he asked inexorably. "Are you?"

Julianne bit her lip and shifted her gaze to his chin. It was dented by a distinct cleft. His voice had sounded cultured. "Yes," she said. "I am."

He stayed where he was for another moment, his face still very close to hers. Then he pushed himself away from the wall. "I thought so," he remarked neutrally. "One doesn't see skin like that in Africa."

Instinctively she raised a hand to her cheek. "Circassians are fair-skinned," she protested defensively. She could breathe more easily now that he had moved away from her.

"I was not referring to your coloring."

"Oh," she said blankly, not having the vaguest idea what he was talking about.

He didn't enlighten her. His thick black hair had fallen forward over his forehead and impatiently he pushed it back. "Will you kindly explain to me what the devil a girl like you is doing in a slave auction in Cairo?" He sounded distinctly irritable.

"Being sold," she returned tartly. She didn't like his tone.

There was a long silence in which they regarded each other, measuringly. Julianne felt her heart begin to hammer again. She was a fool to provoke him, she thought. He looked tough and ruthless as well as dangerous. Then, abruptly, he smiled. "So you were." His voice was surprisingly mild—pleasant even.

The menace she had felt was suddenly gone from the room and she found herself looking at a charming, handsome stranger who sounded exactly like an English gentleman. The change left her feeling a little lightheaded with relief. "It's a long story," she said rather unsteadily, "and I think I need to sit down."

"Have a cushion," he said hospitably. Then, when she dropped down to the floor and bent her head for a minute: "Do you want a glass of wine? Are you going to faint?"

At that she looked up. "No, I am not going to faint."

"Good." He dropped to a cushion himself with an ease that bespoke long familiarity with the ways of the East. "I didn't think you were the fainting type."

"I'm not." She sounded annoyed.

He nodded and there was a faint smile in the brilliant blue-green of his eyes. "Well?" he prompted softly. "I'm listening."

Julianne took a deep even breath, conscious that the tension had left her muscles as well as the room. "My father was an English missionary here in Africa," she began agreeably. "His task was to create a series of mission stations along the East African coast. He was killed by a lion a few months ago in Abyssinia, and the local king, a very unpleasant man who had refused to supply us with porters and bearers, sold me to some Arab slave traders. I was taken to Harar, where I was sold again to a trader who was bringing slaves to Cairo. He was the man who sold me to you."

His face was expressionless. "Not a very pleasant experience," he murmured.

"No. But I had it much easier than the black slaves. They suffered terribly."

"For how long were you and your father in Africa?"

"Five years."

"Five years!" There was profound surprise in

his voice. "Do you mean you have been traveling throughout Africa for five years?"

"Yes."

"Jesus Christ." He stared at her in open astonishment. "You can't be more than eighteen."

"I am nineteen."

"How far did you travel? To Abyssinia?"

"No, we went south as far as Zanzibar."

"On foot?"

"On foot. It is difficult to carry on missionary work from a ship."

He smiled sardonically. "Were you very successful in spreading the Word?"

"We had very little success," she replied serenely. "We did, however, see quite a bit of Africa."

The sardonic note vanished. "I'll bet you did. I'm sure you went where no white man has been before. I envy you." There was no doubting his sincerity. "Who was your father?" he asked curiously. "For that matter, who are you?"

"My father was Lord Richard Wells. I am Julianne Wells."

"Lord Richard Wells. Good God—wasn't he the duke's son who came out a few years ago?"

"Yes."

He pushed the thick hair back out of his eyes again and looked at her with raised brows. "Well, well, well," he said softly. "It isn't often that one finds the granddaughter of a duke at a slave auction."

"No, I suppose not," she agreed evenly. "Nor

does one often find an English gentleman on the puchasing end of such a market."

His mouth quirked a little. "True." Then, as she didn't say anything but continued to regard him steadily, he grinned. "My turn, you think?"

"Yes, I think so."

The smile left his face but still lingered in his eyes as he said, "My name is John Champernoun, Julianne. I came out to Egypt fifteen years ago with the English expedition against Napoleon, and I have been here ever since. At present you might say I am an adviser to the pasha."

"I see," she said slowly. Then she frowned a little in concentration. Hadn't she heard her father speaking once of some "renegade Englishman" who was training Mohammed Ali's armies? "What do you do for the pasha?" she asked cautiously.

"For the past year I've been engaged in helping to put down the Wahabi uprising in Arabia. In fact, I haven't been in Cairo above a week. It was just chance I happened to be at that auction. Khalil Derwish Bey, one of the Mameluke overlords, wished to go, and as I was dining with him I went along to be polite. When I saw you I was convinced you were English."

It sounded very much to Julianne as if John Champernoun were indeed the renegade her father had condemned so roundly. She replied slowly, "I still don't quite understand how you were so certain of that. No one else doubted that I was Circassian. I speak Arabic very well."

"I told you your skin gave you away," he said

in his deep voice. Then, as she opened her mouth to protest again, he continued calmly, "I'm not talking about its color but about its texture. And then, too, there was the expression on your face."

By now she was feeling extremely puzzled. "My expression?"

"Yes. Aloof, withdrawn, *noli me tangere*. You looked"—his white teeth flashed briefly in amusement—"like a snow queen dressed up as a houri. Not at all Circassian."

The corners of Julianne's mouth deepened in acknowledgment. "I was not enjoying myself."

"No, I don't imagine you were." He rose to his feet with easy, animal grace. "Well, I suppose I shall have to see about shipping you home to England. You have someone to go to, I presume."

"Yes, my grandmother." She rose too and was again surprised by how tall he was—taller even than her father had been.

"One thing still puzzles me," he said now. "Why did you conceal the fact that you were English? The pasha is anxious to remain on friendly terms with England. He would have had very good reason to see you safely restored to your noble relations."

She looked at him skeptically. "The last time I was in Cairo, Mr. Champernoun, there was a great deal of admiring talk about how Mohammed Ali had beaten the English at Alexandria and then rode his horse in a triumphal procession between the chained bodies of captive English soldiers who were waiting to be sold into slavery. I did not think my nationality would gain me any sympathy with the pasha or his supporters."

His sunburned features looked grim. "Did you hear that story in Cairo or in London?"

"I . . ." She frowned in concentration and thought back. "It was in London, I suppose," she finally said slowly. "But there was an ugly anti-English sentiment in Cairo when we arrived. Of that I am certain."

"Yes, I can believe that. But I can assure you, Julianne, that there were no English soldiers sold into slavery by the pasha. Mohammed Ali is fully aware of the importance of keeping Britain's goodwill. When Fraser evacuated from Alexandria after the Treaty of Tilsit was signed, the pasha released all the British prisoners who had fallen into his hands. All that were left were the heads of a few decapitated British soldiers which were decorating the pleasure grounds of Ezbekiah. Barbarous, true, but it was not that long ago that we stuck heads up on London Bridge."

"If what you say is true, how did the other story get started in London?"

"Well, for one thing, British public opinion is against Mohammed Ali. He has put down the Mamelukes and the Mamelukes are popular in Britain. The press likes to dwell on their Oriental splendor and the fact that they fought against Napoleon. The fact that they have plundered and raped Egypt for centuries means nothing to the fine British reading public. It would much rather read about how Mohammed Ali eats babies for dinner than about the economic havoc

Mameluke rule has wreaked on Egypt. Christ! Even in the Ottoman dominions it would be difficult to discover a people more oppressed, an economy more decayed."

Julianne was surprised by the bitterness of his voice. "When you first came into the room I thought you were a Mameluke," she said softly.

His mouth tightened and a singularly unpleasant expression crossed his face. "Well, I'm not."

She shivered a little. "I read Volney before we came to Egypt and I remember something he wrote about the Mamelukes. 'Strangers among themselves, they are not bound by the bonds that bind other men. Without parents or children, the past has done nothing for them; they do nothing for the future.' "

"That sums them up perfectly."

She frowned a little. "I do not understand what he means by saying they have no parents or children, though."

"The Mamelukes are children of Christians whose parents sold them into slavery for profit," he explained. "They were trained as a military guard and centuries ago one of the Mameluke captains seized the sultanate and made himself master of Egypt. From then on the Mamelukes ruled in Egypt. The successor of each sultan was usually secured by the violent death of his predecessor. Lesser Mameluke chiefs ruled the provinces under a kind of feudal system. But there was no hereditary system of power. The strong prevailed and the weak fell by the wayside. The ruling passion of the Mameluke is self-interest. He is not Egyptian so he feels no ties to the fellahin of this country. His sons are to him what he was to his father: a threat. The result is that for six hundred years they have held Egypt in a tyranny which nobody in the world, except the very misinformed British government, has ever attempted to condone."

There was no mistaking the genuine disgust in his voice. "And Mohammed Ali is different?" she asked softly.

His straight black brows rose slightly and he looked down at her, a gleam of amusement in his eyes. "He is different. I won't try to tell you he is a great humanitarian, because he's not. But he wants to bring Egypt out of the Middle Ages and into the modern world and he has instituted quite a few necessary reforms."

"And you are helping him?"

"Yes. I am helping him."

"By training his armies?"

His eyes narrowed. "That is one of my duties."

She longed to ask him if he had led the siege against the British in Alexandria, but she didn't quite dare.

"Well, I will be extremely grateful if you can find the means to transport me home to England," she said instead. "My grandmother will repay you for any expenses, I am certain."

He made a dismissive gesture. "It may take a little time for me to make the arrangements. In the meantime I think it would be best if we kept your presence here a secret. If there was a respectable Englishwoman I could turn you over to, I'd do it at once, but there is no one." He gave her a mocking smile. "Your reputation would be irreparably damaged if it became known you were staying with me, I fear."

"Then we must be discreet," she said serenely, meeting his eyes with cool composure.

He smiled a little crookedly. "Not much frightens you, does it, Julie?"

"Not much," she replied with perfect truth. Then she too smiled a little. "But I was frightened when you came into this room. More frightened than I've ever been in my life."

"You didn't look it."

"No. Well, one has one's pride."

"So I gather." He glanced around the room. "You will be perfectly free here in the house to go where you wish. Please make yourself comfortable. I'll have Fatama get you some clothes, although"—and his eyes glinted—"from my point of view what you have on is very nice indeed."

Julianne was immediately conscious of the curves of her body, so clearly visible to his knowing eyes through the thin fabric of her clothing. She felt the telltale color begin to stain her cheeks and her eyes fell. "No one will bother you," he said, an undertone of amusement in the deep pleasant voice. "Just don't go out."

"I won't," she promised. "And thank you, Mr. Champernoun."

"Call me John. We'll probably be seeing a bit of each other in the next few weeks."

He turned to leave and she said quickly, "I left

some things—papers, notes—at the other house. Could you send for them?"

He looked surprised. "However did you manage to hang on to your papers?"

"It wasn't easy."

"No. I'll send Said over there in the morning."

"Thank you," she said. "John."

He smiled a little in acknowledgment but made no reply as he left her alone in the beautiful silken room.

Chapter Five

A path that leads to perill and mishap . . .
        —Sir Walter Ralegh

John Champernoun's house was magnificent, but as she wandered about it, admiring all the beautiful things it contained, Julianne got the distinct impression that he was as transient in it as she was. There was an adequate staff of servants. The house was immaculate and the food appeared regularly, but there was a museumlike quality to the place, she thought. There was no sign of domesticity. The harem was empty.

She mentioned her feeling to Said, one of the men who had escorted her on the night she first came to the house by Lake Ezbekhiah. It seemed that Said was John's chief lieutenant and he also appeared to be a friend. "This is a very beautiful house," she said to him, "but I get the impression that John regards it as little more than a tent where he is making a temporary stay."

Said had looked at her cautiously. He was not

comfortable in her company. He recognized that she must be treated differently from the women to whom he was accustomed, but he was finding it difficult to adapt himself. "He has only owned the house for a short time," he finally answered. "The pasha gave it to him as a reward for his service in Arabia."

Julianne looked for a moment at a priceless vase which adorned one of the low tables in the room where she spent most of her time. "He must have done a very good job indeed," she said dryly.

Said's face became unusually animated. "He recaptured the holy cities of Medina and Mecca. The pasha's armies had been in Arabia for two years before John went out. It was only when he arrived that we began to win. The official leader of the Egyptian army in Arabia is still the pasha's son, Ibrahim, but he knows who is truly responsible for his victories."

"I see."

"Mohammed Ali is leaving for Arabia himself in a few weeks' time to make an official entry into Mecca," Said offered. "It will be a great moment for Islam. And for Egypt."

Julianne felt a pang of anxiety. "Will John be going as well?"

Said looked shocked. "John cannot enter the holy city, lady. He is an infidel."

"Oh," said Julianne. "I see."

John's assertion that they would be seeing a bit of each other was not exactly true, as Julie found out in the following weeks. He was working on her problem, he assured her, whenever she did catch sight of him. There was a Frenchwoman, a Mme. Rioux, he thought could be persuaded to escort her to England. The lady was expected back in Cairo shortly, and he would speak to her then.

It seemed, however, that Julianne was one of the smallest of his problems. He seemed to be in constant motion, and often she would hear him returning to the palace in the early morning. She wondered where he had been, but wasn't quite sure she wanted to know the answer. She had a feeling that the less she knew about his doings the more tranquil she would be.

One evening, after she had been in residence for ten days, Fatama, whom Julianne thought of as the housekeeper, came to tell her that the lord had requested her company at dinner. Julie dressed herself carefully in a pair of full ankle-length trousers and a pretty soft cotton shirt which had been bought for her by Fatama. She did her hair in a long single braid and tied it with a silver ribbon. Then she went downstairs to join her host in one of the rooms that led off the courtyard.

There was a table set for two in the room and next to it, looking out at the fountain, was John Champernoun. He wore Egyptian dress as usual and Julie found herself thinking that the Eastern clothes looked remarkably appropriate on his tall broad-shouldered figure. He turned as she came into the room. "Ah, here you are. I thought it might be pleasant to have dinner together. I was finally able to get away from the citadel for a while."

She smiled politely. "The pasha keeps you busy."

"He does." He held a chair for her and then sat down himself across the table. The servants came in with food and wine and as they ate John asked her about her travels in Africa. She spoke generally at first, but the intensity of his interest led her on. As she talked about their journey inland from Zanzibar the lines of his face sharpened and brightened. "You actually saw a snow-covered mountain near the equator!" he exclaimed in excited amazement.

"Yes. We saw its peak, at any rate. The Masai people called it Ngaje Nga—'House of God.' I shouldn't be surprised if it were over sixteen thousand feet."

"Christ! Julie, do you realize this means that Ptolemy's map may be correct?"

"The Mountains of the Moon, you mean?"

"Yes."

"It may be. I questioned some ivory traders in the area. On Ptolemy's map he had the Nile's sources as two lakes a little south of the equator. According to these traders, there *are* two great lakes. And beyond them a range of mountains."

His face was brilliant, an adventurer's face with glowing light eyes. "Almighty God. What I wouldn't give to have been there."

She took a sip of her wine and watched him over the rim of the glass. "But the Blue Nile

rises at Lake Tana," she said. "James Bruce re-
ported that forty years ago. And when Papa and
I visited the Ethiopian court we saw it for
ourselves."

He leaned toward her, formidable in his intensity. "I know, but the true source of the Nile is
the source of the White Nile, Julie; that is the
longer branch. And no one has found that source.
At least, not yet. I hope you kept a record of all
this? Was that the papers you were so worried
about?"

"Yes. Papa kept a journal."

"And you?"

"Yes," she said with palpable reluctance. "I
did keep a journal."

"Would you let me see it?" His eyes were
glittering, twin aquamarines in his sun-dark face.

She dragged her eyes away from that blazing
look. "They would not interest you. Papa wrote
almost exclusively about his missionary work.
And mine is—well, it is rather personal. Not at
all scientific, I'm afraid." She was slowly revolv-
ing her wineglass, watching the candlelight reflected in the crystal. He said nothing, but she
could feel his eyes on her face. "I wrote mostly
about the animals I observed," she said unwill-
ingly.

"Lion and elephant and what else—hippo?"

"Yes. And waterbuck, impala, wildebeest. Sometimes leopard and rhinoceros. And birds—marvelous, beautiful birds."

"I'd like to see your journal," he repeated and
she looked up from her glass to meet his eyes.

She had never intended to show anyone that journal. It was profoundly important to her.

"All right," she heard herself saying. After a minute she pushed her wineglass toward the center of the table. She didn't want to pick it up again as she was afraid her hand was trembling. "Tell me about the war in Arabia," she said with outward calm. "Who are these Wahabis you were fighting?"

There was a brief pause, but then he answered readily enough, "They are a puritanical Moslem sect who are led at present by the house of Ibn Sa'ud. A few years ago Sa'ud drove out the sherif of Mecca, occupied the holy cities, and declared that the caliphate—the official leadership of Islam—belonged to Arabia and not to Constantinople. The sultan, understandably, did not appreciate this challenge to his power and he asked Mohammed Ali to put down the rebellion. The pasha, as a good vassal, could not refuse."

"What do you mean when you say they are puritanical? How do they differ from the Moslems of Turkey and Egypt?"

He pushed back his chair. "If you've finished eating, let's go outside and I'll tell you."

Obediently she rose and accompanied him out into the lovely garden that filled the large central courtyard of the palace. It was delightfully cool outside. Julie had long since become accustomed to the African heat, but the soft breeze that stirred her cotton shirt felt very pleasant. They walked to the fountain, and she looked up at him as they stopped before the huge marble basin. The moonlight clearly outlined his strong aquiline profile, the line of his hard mouth.

"The Egyptians are largely Shafi Moslems," he began. "It is generally a less rigorous form of religion than that practiced by the Wahabis. One of the major differences between the two sects is that the Shafis believe in saints or prophets and the Wahabis do not. The Shafis venerate the memories of holy men and set up splendid tombs in their honor. They believe, you see, that these saints function as intermediaries between them and God. To the Wahabis such a belief is idolatry. Their campaign in Arabia was largely a crusade against the cult of saints. They smashed venerated tombs in all the major cities of Arabia before the Porte asked Mohammed Ali to take action against them."

He put his hand on the marble rim of the fountain and Julie found herself noticing how beautiful it was: long and finely shaped and strong. Her nerve ends were acutely aware of him, so close beside her in the moonlight. She felt strange, unsettled, and to hide her agitation she said, "It seems a lot of fuss about very little. What harm can there be in venerating the memory of a holy man?"

"Well, it is a practice that can get a little out of hand." There was laughter in his voice and in the corners of his mouth. "There is a story told of a village in South Arabia whose inhabitants were so wicked that they never produced a saint. Consequently, they had no tomb to venerate. In order to rectify the problem they invited a well-known holy man to visit them. They feasted him well, then, as he slept, they murdered him. Next day they built him an especially fine tomb, which became the object of envy among their neighbors."

She stared at his splendid hawklike profile. "Are you serious?"

"That is the story."

She started to laugh. "I suppose I should say 'how terrible,' but it is awfully funny."

He grinned and flicked her cheek with a careless finger. "You are going to be wasted in England, Julie. A true Englishwoman would have been horrified."

She sobered immediately. "I am out of practice at being a 'true Englishwoman,' but I mean to do my best to learn." She stepped a little away from him, uneasy at her reaction to that casual caress.

"You won't succeed," he said positively.

"Why not?"

"To be truly English is to be dull, boring, and hypocritical." He turned to face her. "I don't think you could be any of those things."

"I hope not, but I don't agree with your definition. To be English is to be calm and sane and secure and reasonable."

There was a mocking look on his dark face. "Is that what you want? To be calm and sane and secure and reasonable?"

"Yes," she said decidedly.

He reached out, put his hand on the thick blond braid that fell to her waist, and pulled it until her head tipped back. "Your eyes remind me of lake water," he murmured, "cool, shining, unfathomable. Not reasonable at all." His other hand came up to caress the smooth skin of her throat. He bent his head toward her. She watched the slow, unhurried descent of his mouth with dilated eyes, caught between the hand on her hair and the one on her throat. As his mouth touched hers she stiffened in protest and tried to pull away. The hand that was on her neck moved to her back, pulling her hard against him.

No one within Julie's memory had ever kissed her on the mouth. The initial shock of it was reflected in the rigidity of her body and the way her head strained back against his hand. But after a moment, as his kiss deepened and he refused to let her go, shock began to give way to something else. Her body melted into pliancy and her mouth softened under the hardness of his. She closed her eyes.

When he released her she almost lost her balance and put her hands on his chest to steady herself. The thudding of his heart under the thin cotton of his shirt startled her. She looked up at him, confused by the tumult of her own feelings. "You will be wasted in England," he repeated. Then, putting her away from him gently: "I think you had better go inside before I am tempted to do that again." Without a word she turned and went into the house.

Chapter Six

———

This country swarms with vile outrageous men...
——Christopher Marlowe

Julie was bewildered and aghast by her reaction to John Champernoun's kiss. She could not understand why she had ceased to resist him. She was horribly afraid that she might even have kissed him back!

Consequently, she was stiff and embarrassed the next time they met. He, on the contrary, was cool and brisk and efficient. No one would have been able to tell from his demeanor that last time they were together he had held her in his arms. She found that instead of being grateful for his apparent unconcern, she was annoyed. Then she was annoyed with herself for being annoyed. Really, she thought, as she listened to his incisive voice detailing the way he was planning to deal with her, he was a very irritating man.

"I am going to send you to Alexandria with Said," he told her. "Mme. Rioux is still there and her husband is certain she will not object to undertaking a journey to England. You will leave in three days. Said must be here for the pasha's festival tomorrow."

He seemed suddenly quite anxious to be rid of her, but Julie did not object. "Very well," she said quietly. She was confident that this Mme. Rioux would do as John requested. He was not the sort of man one refused very easily.

"What is this festival about?" she asked as he seemed on the point of turning and leaving.

He swung around a little to face her again. "The pasha's son, Ibrahim, is being invested with the Pelisse of Honor for his part in the retaking of the holy cities. The kislar aga is here from the Porte in order to perform the ceremony. All of the Mameluke lords will be there as well. After the investiture there is to be a great procession from the citadel through the city. Said is to be at the ceremony, along with myself."

"I understood that *you* were the one who engineered the retaking of the holy cities," she said on a note of inquiry.

"The leader of the army was Ibrahim," he replied, his voice without expression. "The victories are his. I should ignore any comments you may hear to the contrary."

"I see. And you have been well rewarded for your part already."

His teeth flashed in acknowledgment. "I have been well rewarded."

Julie sighed. "I should love to see the procession.

If the Mamelukes are taking part it is bound to be splendid."

His black brows snapped together. "You stay away from Cairo tomorrow," he ordered. "I don't want you to leave this house. Is that understood?"

Julianne was a little white around the nostrils. There was an uncomfortable pause, then she said crisply, "To hear is to obey, my lord."

He looked at her assessingly and she stared steadily back. "You had better," he said grimly. "I wouldn't want to be in your shoes if I find out you haven't."

Julie did not disobey. Part of her wanted to, and not just because she would have enjoyed seeing the procession. It was that she was sick and tired of being ordered around. All of her life she had been bullied by an authoritarian male. In many ways Lord Richard had been worse than the Arab slavers to whom she had been sold. Her instinct, when John spoke to her in that voice of grim command, was to rebel.

As a child she had loved her father and had exerted herself to please him. He had not been a neglectful parent and had spent long hours with his only daughter. He taught her Arabic. He drilled her in the Scriptures. She learned a great deal about medicine and injuries. She was allowed little liberty for her own pursuits; from the time she was seven her day had been strictly laid out for her.

Julianne had wanted very much to please him. When he said "go," she went; "come," she came; "do this," she did it. He was not an easy master.

She felt every failure on her part was a personal wound to him, deeply engraved and permanent.

When he had determined to go to Africa, it had not occurred to her that she would not accompany him. It was what he had been training her for during all those years of study. Both she and her mother were his willing satellites, securely under the domination of his formidable, austere, commanding character. When her grandmother had begged to keep Julianne, Lord Richard had said in his measured tones: "Julianne is docile, diligent, faithful, constant, and courageous. Despite her years she is both gentle and heroic; her assistance to me in Africa will be invaluable. There is no question of her staying behind."

Julie had been fourteen and proud of his high opinion of her. When finally they reached Africa she strained to satisfy him until she ached with the effort.

It was only gradually that she became aware that physically her mother was incapable of the task her husband had set for her. She was not strong, but Lord Richard urged her to impossibilities. There was no slowing of their pace, no permission to rest during the hot hours. Julie protested, but her mother exerted herself to do all that he asked of her. She died less than a year after they reached Africa.

After the death of her mother Julie began to see her father with new eyes. She loved the vast silent beauty of Africa, but he did *not* wish her to waste her time with such trivialities as the observation of nature and its beauty. She still wished to please him but to do so she felt daily more and more that she must disown half her nature, stifle half her faculties.

Julie was growing out of childhood. Her father, once the god of her existence, became more and more in her eyes a cold and unbending tyrant. She turned from him into herself, into the spontaneity of her response to the glory of Africa, into her own natural and unenslaved feelings. She began to keep a diary.

Lord Richard responded first with verbal disapproval and then with iron silence. He felt all the anger that an austere and despotic nature must feel when it meets with resistance where it expected submission, when it detects feelings and views with which its cool and inflexible judgment does not sympathize.

It was only when she stood up against her father that Julie realized the measure of the man. Without one overt act of hostility, one upbraiding word, he managed to impress her constantly with the conviction that she had gone beyond the pale of his favor. He was a man of marble. He would accept no olive branches of reconciliation. He would settle for nothing but total capitulation. After a while Julie gave up trying to heal their estrangement. From absolute submission he drove her to determined revolt.

She would not leave him, but they were irrevocably alienated. Julie turned more and more into herself, into the solace of her writing, into the resources within herself she had not known she possessed. And she determined that never again would she allow herself to come under the domination of a hard, implacable, pitiless man such as her father.

So when John Champernoun spoke to her with harsh authority, Julie's impulse was childishly to defy him. But she was not a child and had long since ceased to act on unreflecting impulse. John had told her he was concerned for her reputation, and she understood and appreciated that concern. He was undertaking the trouble and the expense of seeing she was returned to England in safety. She owed him a great deal. If he had not been at that sale. . . . her mind tended to shy away from that dreadful possibility. He had saved her life, she felt, and the least she could do was to obey his wishes. So she did. But it irked her all the same.

Late the following afternoon, the day of the ceremony at the citadel, Julie was sitting reading in the shade in the courtyard when she heard the sound of a commotion outside the house. There was the sound of shouting and the clatter of horses' hooves and she looked up, surprised. Usually the road was very quiet. After a few minutes the noise faded away, and she went back to her book.

She was reading a well-worn copy of Shakespeare which she had borrowed from John's surprisingly extensive book collection. Most of the volumes looked well read, and some, such as the Shakespeare, were definitely travel-stained. The books were about the only possession he owned that seemed personal.

Julie was blissfully devouring as much as she could of his library. Her father's idea of suitable reading material had been confined to the *Bible*, *Pilgrim's Progress*, and Foxe's *Book of Martyrs*. John had books on history, travel, and—surprising to her—a great deal of poetry. Julie went through the Elizabethan poets with relish, gobbled up the blood-and-passion plays of Marlowe, Webster, and Tourneur, and then she found Shakespeare. The book hadn't been with the others when she first started to read, and she thought that John must have had it and put it back when he realized what she was doing. Reading Shakespeare was like opening a door on a marvelous new world, and consequently she paid little attention to the unusual disturbance and went happily back to *Othello*.

Half an hour later there was another disturbance and this time Said came rushing into the courtyard. "You must come inside, lady," he said urgently. "John said you must go upstairs to your room and keep out of sight. There may be danger."

"What has happened?" Julie asked, rising to do as he requested.

"There has been an incident at the citadel. Mohammed Ali ordered the massacre of all the Mamelukes. Even now the soldiers are searching the city for any survivors. They will certainly come out to Ezbekhiah. John thinks this house will be safe, but he wants you to remain hidden. I have a guard of men stationed outside. Please do not worry."

"Dear God!" Julie was hurrying along beside

him as he spoke. "Is John all right?" she asked as they reached her room.

"Of course. He is waiting to see the pasha and and then he will return here. Please do not be afraid."

"No, I won't be afraid. Go now, Said. I promise I will stay right here." He looked at her, a tinge of admiration in his dark eyes, and then he went.

All through the long hours that followed, Julie was aware of the soldiers on the road outside the house. It was not until the dawn was beginning to break that a tap came on the door of her room. She had not been to bed, had not even changed her clothes. "Come in," she said instantly. The door opened and it was John.

Her initial feeling was a rush of wild relief. "Thank God you are all right!" she said. "I have been so worried. What happened?"

He came into the room and for the first time she caught a glimpse of his face. The look in his eyes frightened her, as did the grim set of his mouth. With an odd sensation of shock she realized he was very angry. When he spoke there was a cold stillness in his voice that made her shiver a little. "Are you all right?" He ignored her own question.

"Yes. I have been in this room since Said returned this afternoon. The road has been busy but no one has come into the house."

"They had better not have."

Julie stared at him; he looked like a stranger. Then she said softly, "John, please. What happened? I don't know."

It seemed as if he saw her for the first time. "Didn't Said tell you?"

"He told me that the pasha had ordered a massacre of the Mamelukes. That is all."

He laughed harshly. "That is quite enough. There were over four hundred and fifty of them at the citadel today. All dead now. The soldiers are breaking into houses all over Cairo searching for the Mamelukes who were not at the ceremony. The city looks as if it's been sacked."

She stared at him with horrified eyes. "How did it happen?"

"It was during the ceremonial procession," he said in a more normal voice. He ran his hand through his already disordered hair. "In order to leave the citadel the procession had to move down a narrow passage cut into the rock which leads to one of the outer gates. There are high walls and buildings on either side of the passage. The pasha's troops went first, in an orderly succession, but when the Janissaries had passed through the wall and into the square outside, the gate was suddenly shut. Only the Albanians and the Mamelukes were left inside. The Albanians turned and opened fire at the same time that a fusillade was poured at the Mamelukes from the walls above. They were trapped. The passage is narrow. The horses went wild. When it was over the passage looked like a butcher's shambles."

Julie pressed shaking hands to her mouth. "He had it completely planned," she breathed.

"Yes, he did, the murderous bastard. I knew something was in the wind. I could sense it. But this!" He paced to the window and looked out. "It's one thing to kill a man in battle, Julie, but to butcher him in cold blood." He sounded savage.

"Did you see the pasha?"

He laughed harshly. "No. He wouldn't see me."

"He will wait until you are less angry," she said. At that he turned and looked at her. "Why did he do it, John? Do you know?"

"Oh, his reason is clear enough. He did not want to go to Arabia and leave them an open field. The Mamelukes have never been reconciled to Mohammed Ali. So he decided to get rid of them."

"Who knew about the scheme? Just the Albanians?"

"Yes. Obviously he did not want me to know and they're the only part of the army he could trust to hold their tongues."

"Of course he didn't want you to know," she said calmly. "He knew you wouldn't approve. It needs an Eastern mind to appreciate a scheme like that."

"Precisely. That is why it was so stupid! The pasha needs more than anything at this moment to be on good terms with England. If England thinks he has plans to dominate the entire area, she will take alarm. She will be worried about India. Mohammed Ali cannot rule in Egypt without the goodwill of England. And the English do not have Eastern minds."

"I see," she said a little dryly. "You are upset because it was not politically expedient for the pasha to massacre hundreds of Mamelukes."

His face hardened. "No, it was not. As I would have told him had he confided his plans to me."

"I expect that is why he did not. He didn't want to hear it."

The line of his mouth was uncompromising and grim. "No, he did not. But he is going to hear it now. Whether he likes it or not." He seemed to notice for the first time that she was still wearing day clothes. "Go to bed, Julie. The worst is over."

"Yes," she said in reply. "I will."

After he had gone she was conscious of a great feeling of relief that Mohammed Ali and not she was on the receiving end of John's temper. Thank God she had not gone into Cairo today!

Chapter Seven

For I protest before God, there is none, on the
face of the yearth, that I would be fastened
unto.

—Sir Walter Ralegh

For two days after the massacre the hunt continued and Mameluke property was sacked. In Cairo
alone about 4,000 Mamelukes were slain and the
pasha gave orders to all provincial governors to
search out and annihilate any who remained. Mohammed Ali was now the undisputed master of
all Egypt.

Julie saw nothing of John for almost a week
after the massacre. She understood that for him
her problem had receded to the background and
philosophically she decided that he would get to
her when he had the time. She went back to her
books.

She was reading in the courtyard when he
finally sought her out one afternoon. She looked
up and was surprised to find him standing there

watching her. "How long have you been there?" she asked, laying her book aside.

"Not very long. What are you reading?"

"The Tempest." She folded her hands in her lap and looked serenely up at him.

He smiled faintly and came to sit beside her. "Did you think I had forgotten you?"

"No. I thought you were probably very busy."

He sighed, leaned his head back against the wall, and closed his eyes. "You are a remarkable girl, Julie. You don't panic and you don't make unreasonable demands. Remarkable."

Julie studied his face in silence for a moment. He looked very tired. There was a long silence which she did not disturb and then he opened his eyes again. "You will be leaving for England tomorrow," he said. "I don't imagine you have a tremendous amount of packing to do."

"It shouldn't take me very long at all," she agreed with infinite calmness. "Have you located Mme. Rioux?"

"You are not going to travel with Mme. Rioux. You are traveling with me."

There was a pause of utter astonishment, then Julie said, "You?"

"Me. The pasha wants me to undertake a mission to England. It seems that only I am capable of persuading the British government that his massacre of the Mamelukes and his triumphs in Arabia do not mean that he has designs on India."

"Good heavens. Then you convinced him that he was in danger of alienating England?"

"Yes," he said with weary irony, "I did." He closed his eyes again.

This time she did break the silence. "What kind of a man is Mohammed Ali, John?"

He stretched his long legs in front of him and answered in a roundabout fashion. "Two years ago the pasha was riding through a small provincial town, when a baker approached him and complained of the ill-usage he had suffered at the hands of the local governor. Mohammed Ali sent for the governor and had him pitched into the baker's oven, where he was slowly roasted to death." He turned his head and looked at her. "That is the kind of man he is."

"*Was* the local governor corrupt?" she asked slowly.

"Absolutely. They all were, I'm afraid."

"I see. In England I believe we call actions like the pasha's 'Jedburgh justice.'"

He grinned. "I believe you are right. The number of bad characters the pasha has hanged without trial is enormous, but it is far surpassed by the host of poor men whose wrongs he has righted. And he is the first ruler in Egypt for centuries who is trying to improve the agricultural base of the country. He has set in motion irrigation projects that should double the amount of crops the fellahin can raise."

"That is certainly a good thing. But he is ruthless, is he not?"

"Yes. He has no regard whatsoever for human life."

"Yet you have worked for him for years."

"He's a cunning bastard, but I like him." A sardonic note crept into his voice. "We probably have a lot in common."

"Probably," she agreed, and he laughed and rose to his feet.

"We leave for Alexandria tomorrow at seven."

"I shall be ready," she said. He stretched the muscles of his back as if they felt cramped from lack of exercise, nodded to her absently, and went into the house. After a minute, Julie picked up her book again.

They went by boat to Alexandria, where they boarded one of the pasha's prized new naval vessels. The Egyptian winter weather was lovely, cool and comfortable, and the temperature remained cool but pleasant as they proceeded through the Mediterranean. Julie enjoyed sitting on deck wrapped in the wide, loose cloak of very fine white wool that John had presented her with. It was of Arabian rather than Egyptian style, and all its borders were worked in a beautiful elaborate pattern of colored silks. She braided her hair securely in a thick plait so it would not blow, and wore no headdress. The area where she sat was off limits to the seamen, who, as good Moslems, never thought of intruding into her isolation.

And, for the most part, she was isolated. She saw very little of John. It was a small ship and he could not have that much to occupy him, Julie found herself thinking rather frequently. She suspected that he was avoiding her.

About halfway through the journey he asked to borrow her journals. Since Julie had been reading his books for several months at this point, she hardly felt she could refuse. She was sitting on deck two days later when he appeared with the worn-looking notebooks in his hands. He sat down in a chair, propped his feet on the rail, and regarded her speculatively. His long fingers moved lightly up and down the discolored red cover of her book. "This is a remarkable document," he said seriously.

Julie felt herself flushing. "I thought you might find it silly."

He looked astonished. "I never read anything less silly in my life. Africa comes alive in these pages. You make it live and breathe in a way no one else has ever done. No one else who has your literary talent has ever *been* to Africa. Certainly no European has seen what you have recorded here. I think you should publish it."

"Do you really think it is that good?" Julie could hear the breathless excitement in her own voice.

In answer he opened the book at random and read: " 'All night long restless lions could be heard on both sides of the river. The air was filled with the smell of animals, and in a moment's silence there came the screech of a hyena, eerie and excited as it tore to pieces its unfortunate prey.' " He looked up. "You loved Africa, didn't you?"

"Yes."

He nodded. "You make it come alive," he repeated. "When you get to England you should see about getting this published." He looked directly into her eyes. "I am serious, Julie."

She felt absolutely radiant. She would never have dared to tell anyone what writing had come to mean to her. His recognition of that something in herself that she had secretly believed in and nurtured was one of the most wonderful things that had ever happened to her. "My father thought I was wasting my time," she confessed.

"You weren't." He stayed where he was, lounging in his chair, his feet on the rail, his black hair blowing in the breeze. "I read your father's notes as well." His voice was noncommittal. "No doubt the missionary society will find them of interest. I didn't."

Julie stared at the water. "Papa walked through Africa like a blind man. He never saw how beautiful it was."

"No," he agreed. "From his journal one gathers that he was preoccupied with two things: himself and Jesus."

Julie looked for a minute at John's relaxed body, his calm, splendid profile. "I think I hated him," she said in a low voice.

He didn't move. "I should imagine you must have. You had utterly opposing temperaments."

She heaved an enormous sigh of relief. "Doesn't anything ever shock you, John?"

At that he turned to look at her. "What should I be shocked about?"

"It is a terrible thing to hate your father. It is a sin."

"Well, if it's a sin, it's certainly a common

one." He grinned at her astonished expression. "I hated mine, too," he offered. "Only in my case it was my uncle rather than my father. My parents died when I was very young and I was placed in the care of my father's elder brother. He was the Earl of Denham and I hated him passionately."

"Why?"

"Oh, he didn't beat me or anything as vulgar as that. He was just so dull, so dreary, so pedantic— and so hypocritical. Everything he touched he blighted. And my cousins were just as bad. I was wild to get away. They were just as anxious to get rid of me, I may add. When a friend of my uncle's was persuaded to find me a position with our embassy in Constantinople, we parted ways with mutual enthusiasm. I had wanted an army commission, but he wouldn't buy me one. As it turned out, the job in Constantinople was the best thing that ever happened to me."

Her eyes were still on his profile. "Tell me about it."

He rose to his feet, put the notebooks on his chair, and went to lean on the rail. "There isn't a whole lot to tell. I wasn't in Constantinople that long—just long enough to pick up some Turkish and some Arabic. I've always been a quick study at languages. That was why Sir Sidney Smith took me to Egypt with him. I remained with Sir Sidney for a few years and when the British finally pulled out, I stayed."

She came and joined him at the rail. "Is this the first time you've been back to England since you left?"

"Yes."

"Don't you miss it at all?"

"No." His dark lashes were lowered, staring down at the water, concealing his eyes. "In England everyone is expected to conform to the same dull mold. In Egypt one has room to breathe. I like the freedom of being able to do what I want to do, be what I want to be, with no one pushing the god of respectability down my throat."

"But don't you miss having a real home?"

He shrugged a little. "Home is wherever night finds me, and that suits me just fine."

She stared down at her hands, which were gripping the rail tightly. "You sound just like my father. He could not—he would not—renounce his dream of mission warfare for the safety and the peace of Crewe Rectory. He was incapable of any of the domestic ties that ordinary people feel, that bind together families and societies."

"Then why did he marry?" His voice sounded harsh and she raised her eyes to his face. He had turned and was looking at her, his eyes hooded and unreadable.

"I imagine he thought my mother would be useful to him," she answered with a trace of bitterness. "He couldn't have loved her. If he had, he would never have brought her to Africa. She wasn't strong. She went because she loved him and she desired, above all else, to please him." The bitterness was more pronounced now, in her voice and in the curve of her mouth. "I will never," said Julianne with deadly certainty, "marry a man like my father."

"A man like your father, a man like myself, ought never to marry." There was an edge on his voice that told her she had hit a nerve. "Women have no concept of personal freedom." His blue gaze flicked angrily across her face. "Even you," he said. "You have traveled where no European has been before, you have seen places and things that most of us have only dreamed of, you have the talent to produce something like this"—he gestured to her journal—"and yet all you can talk about is safety, security, and domestic ties. Christ!" He turned back to the water, his profile like granite.

Julie was furious. "Personal freedom! Don't talk to me about personal freedom!" Her voice was shaking. "It is only another way of being selfish. In pursuing your own great vision, you heroes of personal freedom trample pitilessly on the feelings and the claims of all the little people who look up to you, who depend on you. There is nothing in the world as utterly ruthless as a man who is intent on pursuing his own personal freedom, whether it be as missionary or mercenary. I'm sick of it!" She was white with temper, her eyes blazing as she stared defiantly up at him.

The air between them vibrated with angry tension. Then, "Are you, by God," he said in a breathless, goaded undertone, and pulled her into his arms.

The bruising pressure of his mouth on hers caused Julie to push desperately at his chest, trying to free herself. He only held her more tightly and with the hardness of his mouth he forced her own lips open. After a minute his kiss became more gentle, slow, deliberate and quite astonishingly effective. Her hands were still braced against his chest, but they had ceased to push. After a moment, as the slow erotic kiss continued, they moved up to circle his neck. She was bent back in his embrace and his lips finally left her mouth to move slowly along her exposed throat. "Julie," he murmured, "I have been trying to stay away from you for weeks."

It took a moment for the sound of his words to penetrate Julie's hazy consciousness. "I'd like to get rid of this damn cloak," he said and at that she broke away from him. She retreated from the rail until her back was up against the ship's side.

"Don't touch me!" She was breathing much faster than usual. "Don't come near me."

His eyes were open and brilliantly, intensely blue. He said nothing. After a minute she turned and fled down the stairs to her cabin.

Chapter Eight

For what we sometyme were we are no more . . .
— Sir Walter Ralegh

Julie was deeply shaken by her encounter with
John. She knew about sex, of course. Africans
regarded it as perfectly natural, and she had
seen and heard things that girls of her age in
England were strictly guarded from. But, untouched and unawakened as she was, she had
always regarded it as degrading and rather
repulsive. When she thought of marriage and a
husband, she thought in terms of home and
children. How those children were conceived did
not enter into her fantasies.

John had changed that. She had to admit to
herself that she did not find his kisses at all
repulsive. Quite the contrary. It frightened her,
the way he made her feel. When he had said he
wanted her robe out of the way, she had felt too
the longing for his touch on her bare flesh. It was
that desire which had frightened her into push-

ing away from him and fleeing to the safety of her own room.

He had said he was trying to stay away from her. The thought that she had the power to disturb him, as he did her, pleased her. But she thought it would be best for all concerned if she assisted him in carrying out his prudent course of action. She did not want to fall in love with John Champernoun! The very idea was absurd, she told herself. He was the last man in the world for her. She did not need to give her heart to someone who espoused the creed of "personal freedom." She had seen through that philosophy, thank you. It brought only heartache and despair.

Said came to return her journals the following day. She invited him to sit with her on the deck for a while, and, rather to her surprise, he accepted. What she did not know was that John's temper had been so vile all day that Said found even the company of this strange woman preferable. And Said had secretly admired Julianne ever since the night of the massacre, when she had been so calm and so unafraid.

So he sat beside her now in the bright December sun and talked in a more comfortable manner than he would have thought possible. At a little pause in their conversation Julie brought up the very name she was trying to banish from her thoughts. "Why are there no women in John's house, Said?" Her voice was casual, her face idly curious. Julie had learned well how to mask her feelings.

"He has never had any women in his harem," replied Said, shaking his head at the strangeness of it. "It is not that he is one who likes men," he added, lest she misinterpret his statement. "John is a man for women."

"I don't doubt that," said Julianne dryly.

"It is that he does not want any women of his own. He likes them only briefly."

Julie's nostrils quivered. "Otherwise they might interfere with his personal freedom," she said with palpable sarcasm.

Said missed her irony. "Exactly," he replied, pleased to find her so understanding. "At one time he said to me that once a woman in your harem has a baby, you are saddled with her for life. And women always seem to be having babies."

"It's a good thing for him his mother shared in that failing," Julie said tartly and Said laughed.

"That is true, lady," he agreed, amused by her wittiness. Julie changed the topic of conversation and after another ten minutes Said left, rather reluctantly. John's tongue had been very unpleasant of late.

Said's words had only confirmed Julianne's opinion of her rescuer's character. He *was* her rescuer, she told herself, and for that she must always be grateful to him. But once they landed in England she wanted nothing more to do with him. She would banish him from her mind.

It was not quite so easy to put him out of her

thoughts on the ship. She heard his voice and
caught sight of his tall figure too often for her
peace of mind. And even his books did not serve
to distract her as they once had. The well-worn
poetry, particularly, seemed to echo with his
imprint. Thomas Wyatt appeared to have been
one of his favorites. Certain lines were under-
lined with decisive strokes and Julie read them
again and again, pondering:

> I cannot speak and look like as a saint;
>> Use wiles for wit, or make deceit a pleasure
> And call craft counsel, for profit still to paint.

She thought of what he had said of his uncle
and his hypocrisy. Perhaps, she thought, there
was reason for John to be the way he was. There
were some lines of Ralegh's too that he had
marked:

> Say to the court, it glows
>> And shines like rotten wood;
> Say to the church, it shows
>> What's good, and doth no good:

> Tell men of high condition
>> That manage the estate,
> Their purpose is ambition,
>> Their practice only hate:

If that was how he felt about England and the
English, then his long sojourn in Egypt made
perfect sense. He had not wanted to make this

trip home; she had seen that in his face. Perhaps, she thought shrewdly, he was afraid to return. Perhaps he did not want to find out that his grievances had, after all, no basis in fact.

They landed at Harwich in England. Crewe was only twenty miles from the town, but John installed Julie at an inn. "Neither of us can appear anywhere until we get some Western clothes," he said firmly and Julie had agreed. She was so accustomed to Eastern dress that the dark, heavy clothing she saw on her brief trip from the ship to the inn looked ugly and uncomfortable, but she knew her grandmother would be scandalized by her trousers.

There was a roaring fire in her room at the King's Inn and she huddled gratefully before it for most of the afternoon. Julianne was no longer accustomed to the English climate and thought with definite longing of the steamy heat of Africa.

John came back late in the afternoon and knocked at her door. When she opened it he was holding a large package in his hands. "This is for you," he said and walked past her into the bedroom.

Julie scarcely looked at the parcel which he had laid upon the bed. She was too busy staring at him in his new clothing. He saw her look and grinned sardonically. "Do I look like an English gentleman?"

"No," she replied positively.

His black brows rose. "Why? The tailor assured me that I would look just like everyone else."

Julie shook her head, amused and forgetting to be cautious. "You will never look like everyone else, John." Then, realizing abruptly that they were alone, she asked hastily, "Are those clothes for me? Will we be going to Crewe now?"

His face became very grave. "Julie, you and I need to have a talk."

"About what?" she asked suspiciously.

"About how we are going to deal with the fact that you have been unchaperoned and in my company for several months now."

"But no one knows that."

"If you and I turn up at Crewe together, with no chaperon in sight, people are damn well going to suspect." His voice was as calm as hers.

"Oh," said Julie. They were standing with the width of the room between them, John near the fire and Julie near the door. She moved a little into the room and began to fiddle with the strings on her parcel of clothes. "What do you suggest?" she asked a little nervously.

"I suggest that you change into that dress and come downstairs to have dinner with me. I've hired a private parlor. We can plot strategy over a meal."

She didn't think it was a safe idea, having dinner alone with him. She opened her mouth to object but what came out instead was, "All right."

He nodded briskly and moved past her to the

door. "I'll see you in half an hour," he directed as he left the room.

Julie sighed as the door closed behind him. "Now why did I do that?" she muttered to herself. She began to open her parcel, knowing full well the reason was that after tomorrow she would probably never see him again. She wanted a few more hours of his company before she had to say good-bye. "I must be mad," she decided as she shook out a wool dress of a very pretty shade of blue.

The dress fit fairly well, but the heavy material and the confining skirt felt very strange after the soft cottons and loose trousers she had been wearing. She brushed out her hair, braided it in a single plait, and went downstairs to dinner.

There were other people in the inn's dining room, but the landlord came over to Julie and escorted her to another room further down the hall. When she came in the door, she saw that there was a table set for two, and John was standing with his back to her, looking out the window. She had a sudden feeling of recognition: Just so had he stood, looking out at the courtyard, on the night of their first dinner together. The night he had first kissed her.

"Good evening," she said, in a slightly breathless voice, and he turned to look at her.

"I liked your trousers better," he said after a pause, and she laughed.

"You know, I did too."

He came to hold her chair for her and once she

was seated the waiter came in with the soup.

They talked harmlessly of neutral topics while the initial courses were being served. When the main part of the meal, a joint of roast beef, had been placed on the table, John dismissed the waiter and told him not to return until he was rung for. As the waiter obediently departed, Julie stared at her laden plate. "I can't remember ever having seen so much food at one meal! Surely the English don't eat like this all the time?"

"I suppose they do," said John, regarding his own plate. "I ordered the beef; the rest of the dishes must be standard fare." He looked up at her, a faint smile in his eyes. "The waiter just asked me if we would want some ham and fowl as well."

"You're joking me," she said incredulously. "After soup, salmon, turbot, and now roast beef!"

"I tell you what, Julie," said John, picking up his knife and fork and tucking in. "You've turned into an Easterner. You like wearing trousers and you miss your frugal meals. Would you rather have grilled impala than this very handsome roast beef?"

"Well, perhaps not grilled impala—though it *is* very good," she murmured, picking up her own knife and fork. They ate for a few minutes in silence and then both put down their forks at the same time, looked at each other, and broke into laughter.

John poured himself some wine. "The only thing I have missed about England is the roast beef," he said, shaking his head ruefully. "And I'm too full to enjoy it."

"We shouldn't have eaten so much earlier," she said, picking up her own glass. "But I was hungry then!"

He leaned back in his chair and looked at her across the candlelit table. "Now," he said, "about our problem."

She sobered immediately. "Is it really a problem? Will anyone really care about how I got back to England?"

"You've been away too long, Julie." His voice was lightly sardonic.

"Perhaps." She compressed her lips a little. "Have you any suggestions?"

"I think so." His face was perfectly expressionless as he looked at her across the table. "I will go to see your grandmother tomorrow. I will explain the situation to her and ask that she send some reputable woman here to chaperon you for our arrival at Crewe. I suggest we say that you have come from France, where you were taken by some respectable Frenchwoman in whose care you have been since your father's death."

"I see." Her eyes, staring back at him, were equally expressionless. "It sounds all right to me."

"Do you want me to tell your grandmother the story about the Frenchwoman or the truth?"

Julie's eyes left his and moved to the fire. She thought for a minute and then said, "The truth, I think. At least that part of the truth. If one is going to deceive someone, it is always wiser to stick as close to the truth as is possible."

He shook his head in mock disillusionment. "So young to be so corrupt. And you look as pure and honest as a saint from heaven."

"It's a great help," she answered smoothly. "But don't tell my grandmother about my being sold as a slave, John. And don't tell her about the lion. Say that my father died of fever."

"Oh, so I am the one who is to break the sad news to her?"

"You'll have to, won't you?" She sounded suddenly very tired. "After all, you've got to account for my return."

He was watching her steadily, his eyes slightly narrowed. "Don't worry about it." The mockery had completely left his voice. "I'll tell her. And I will spare her sensibilities about the slave market and the lion. And I will arrange for a chaperon so that you may return home with perfect respectability. I realize," he said unexpectedly, "that none of this has been easy for you. But it's almost over."

For some reason she could not fathom the beat of her heart began to accelerate. "I do not know if I have ever thanked you for all you have done for me," she said hurriedly. "I owe you a great deal, and I am not ungrateful."

"I don't want your gratitude," he said roughly, and her heart beat even faster. She rose to her feet.

"Well, then, I won't bore you with my protestations any longer. But I meant what I said."

He did not rise with her. "That is nice to know." His dark strongly carved face was settled in harsh angles. "Good night, Julie," he said.

She did not want to leave him. "Good night," she replied with calm dignity, and walked out the door.

Chapter Nine

I shall the effect of this good lesson keep
As watchman to my heart.
                    —William Shakespeare

He left for Crewe early next morning and Julie filled up the day as best she could. John had sent the ship and its crew, headed by Said, on to Dover with orders to Said to join him in London in four days' time. Consequently, Julie was by herself at the inn as she waited for John to return with his "respectable" chaperon.

He did not come back until very late in the day. It had grown dark outside when he tapped at her door and she was beginning to worry that something had gone wrong. She felt a great surge of relief at the sight of his tall broad-shouldered figure in the doorway.

"I was afraid you had deserted me," she said with an attempt at lightness, stepping aside and holding the door wide for him to enter. "Did you see my grandmother?"

He came across the threshold, his eyes raking the room. "Yes, I saw her. She was going to send a Mrs. Brightling. Hasn't she arrived yet?"

Julie smiled with pleasure. "My old nurse! No, she has not arrived yet."

"Oh, Christ," said John rudely.

Julie thought she knew what was wrong with him. "You—did you tell my grandmother about Papa?"

"Yes."

She spoke gently, ignoring his bad temper. "I'm sorry you had so unpleasant a task. It cannot have been an enjoyable day."

He shrugged a little as if it was of no importance. "Mrs. Brightling should be here shortly. I have ordered dinner to be served for both of you in the parlor at eight. We are leaving for Crewe tomorrow at nine o'clock and I would like you to be ready on time, please."

She was disconcerted by his brisk, impersonal manner and asked in a bewildered voice, "But won't I see you at dinner?"

"No." He did not elaborate on his answer.

She said nothing, but regarded him gravely as he stood by the door; he had not come very far into the room. For a long silent minute they looked at each other, then John spoke in his clipped, decisive voice. "I want you to know that I meant what I said about your journal. I want you to see about getting it published."

She smiled a little stiffly and made a dismissive gesture. "I did not write it for publication."

He frowned and came a few steps closer to her.

"Yes, you did," he contradicted her. "And it *ought* to be published. It is a very important record of a part of the world that is unknown in Europe. It is well written, the product of a keenly observant and deeply reflective mind." She flushed a little with pleasure. "I want you to promise me you won't turn coward about this. Promise me you will see a publisher."

There was a distinct note of command in his voice, but strangely it did not put her back up. She moved closer to him, inexorably drawn by the strength in his voice and the compelling brilliance of his gaze. "All right," she said softly. "I promise."

There were only two steps between them now and Julie was conscious of the treacherous quickening of the blood she always seemed to feel when she was near him. I won't see him alone again, she thought. I must say something. He seemed to be moving toward her and, with a naturalness that didn't seem at all odd at the time, she went into his arms.

She let him kiss her, her lips warm and yielding under his, her body soft and pliant in his embrace. The kiss became harder, more hungry, and Julie's mouth opened under his demand. She was aware of nothing in the world but the two of them, and the white heat of passion that had ignited between them. His hands were moving over her body. She easily could have pulled free of him had she wanted to. One hand touched her breast and moved caressingly; Julie shuddered with pleasure. He seemed to freeze at the small sound she made and then she felt his hands, hard and hurting, on her shoulders. He put her away from him with rough abruptness and held her that way for a minute before releasing her. The marks of his fingers would be on her shoulders the next morning. "Christ, Julie." His voice was barely recognizable. "Another minute of this and I'll have you down on that bed."

What shocked Julie most of all was the realization that she would like him to do just that. She raised trembling hands to her mouth. "I don't understand what is happening," she whispered.

He laughed, a short harsh sound. She could see the effort he was making to control his breathing. "No? Well, I understand it very well. Why do you think I stayed away from here all day? I only came back when I thought that damn nursemaid would be here."

"Oh." The word was a small breathless sound in the tension-filled room.

He put his hand on the doorknob. "I'll see you in the morning," he said very grimly. He pulled the door open and then slammed it behind him with a violence that caused the lamp on a nearby table to shake. Julie fought down an almost overwhelming desire to burst into tears, and by the time Mrs. Brightling arrived half an hour later she had herself calm and in control.

She was in control the following morning as well. She and her old nurse rode in the carriage the duchess had provided and John rode before them on horseback. They had no opportunity for any private conversation before she was facing him in her grandmother's drawing room to say good-bye.

He called her Miss Wells and offered her his best wishes for her future happiness. She followed his lead, thanked him for all his trouble, and bade him farewell in a cool and stately fashion that utterly belied her actual feelings. As she watched his tall black-haired figure walk out of her grandmother's door and out of her life, she felt lost and deserted and alone.

She remembered that feeling now, as she sat before the dying fire on the night of her come-out ball. She remembered it and she thought she could understand why she had felt so. She thought she could understand what his terrible attraction for her had been.

She had been through a profoundly frightening experience and he had rescued her. There had been no one else to turn to, no one else who cared. Of course she had become dependent on him; of course she had been attracted to him; of course she had almost fancied that she loved him.

From the objective standpoint of several months later, she looked at what had been the situation between them, looked coldly, clearly, measuringly. Her defenses had been down and she had been vulnerable to the attraction of a powerful, good-looking man who had rescued and protected her. In her present objective mood she gave him credit for not taking advantage of her vulnerability. She was honest enough to admit that she had been most terribly vulnerable. But that was the case no longer. She could meet John Champernoun now without a qualm. Now that she had recovered her balance it would be impossible for her to find him attractive. He was utterly opposed to her and to all she held valuable. Her feelings had all stemmed from her own fear and insecurity. She was unlikely ever to see him again, but even if she did she was safe. John Champernoun was not what she wanted out of life.

The fire had burned out and the room was cold but still Julie did not seek the warmth of her bed. She thought now of the ball and the society into which her grandmother had introduced her that evening. That was not what she wanted either: parties, chatter, gossip, flirtations. She wanted a quiet life; a safe marriage with someone with whom she had things in common. She wanted children. She wanted a home. She wanted what she had never had: domestic tranquillity. John had scorned her for such an ambition, but Julie knew that happiness for her lay in calm, in serenity, in absorption in the small things of life that so few people noticed and appreciated.

To get all those things she needed the proper man. There had been many young men at her grandmother's ball, and many of them had looked at her with admiration in their eyes. She would have to begin paying attention to those young men. John Champernoun and Egypt and Africa were in the past. It was the future she must look to now. She went to bed with this thought very firmly in her mind. She knew what she wanted and she was determined to see about getting it. Although she would never have admitted it, Julie could be every bit as ruthless as Lord Richard.

Chapter Ten

> Fain would I wed a fair young man
> That night and day could please me . . .
> —Thomas Campion

There were few who would dispute that the London season of 1815 belonged to Julianne Wells. She was, unquestionably, the loveliest, most-sought-after girl in all the ton that spring. Most of the young men were camped on her doorstep and it was generally agreed that she could have her pick of half a dozen of England's most eligible bachelors, at least two of them hardened cases in their thirties whom most matchmaking mamas had despaired of years ago.

The Dowager Duchess of Crewe was in her element, enjoying herself more than she had in years. She was truly fond of her granddaughter, was proud of her success, and anxious for her to make a wise choice for her future husband. She thought that Julianne would; she appeared to be a girl with a remarkably level head.

The suitor whom the betting at the clubs heavily favored was Lord Rutherford. This young man was good-looking, likable, and his father was the Earl of Minton, one of the greatest nobles in the kingdom. One day Lord Rutherford himself would be the Earl of Minton—immensely powerful, immensely wealthy. The odds makers thought he was a prize few girls would be likely to resist. The odds went up even higher in his favor when the Earl and Countess of Minton paid an unusual visit to town for a week in early June. The ostensible reason for their visit was to attend a party at Carlton House, but the interested ton thought it knew better. They had come to take a look at Julianne Wells. When it became known that the Dowager Duchess of Crewe and her granddaughter were going to Minton for a visit, the odds in the clubs went out of sight. No one was ready to bet against what all now perceived to be a sure thing.

Julie did in fact like Lord Rutherford. She liked his gentle voice and his warm brown eyes. There was a certain mixture of natural modesty and easy courtesy about him that she thought would always keep him from the faults of pomposity and arrogance—faults she had been quick to detect in more than one of her noble suitors. Lord Rutherford, she thought, was a thoroughly nice man and when his mother invited her to pay a visit to Minton, she had about half-decided to marry him if she liked his home.

The Dowager Duchess of Crewe and her granddaughter arrived at Minton on a lovely June afternoon. Julie fell in love with the house before she even walked in the door. Set in the countryside of Kent, it was built of mellow golden stone and looked warm and welcoming in the June sun. The hundreds of windows sparkled. The lawns were richly green, the flower beds a riot of color. And the inside of the house was just as attractive to her. It was elegant and imposing, but it was also clearly a home. The state apartments were awesome, but the family rooms were full of sporting prints and comfortable chairs and her bedroom was decorated with chintz and flowers. It was a house where one felt immediately at ease.

One of the chief reasons for the friendly attraction of Minton was its owner. William Foster, seventh Earl of Minton, was one of the great men of his time. He was both distinguished and unceremonious, rustic and scholarly. He did not greatly care for London and spent the great part of his time in the country, breeding horses, running his estates, collecting art. He was married to a woman whom he dearly loved and had three sons to add to his happiness.

Julie loved Lord Minton. He was the father she had never had: kind and paternal, easygoing and knowledgeable. She loved Lady Minton, so gracious, so friendly, so peaceful. She loved the house and the grounds. It was no wonder that she very soon convinced herself that she loved Lord Rutherford as well.

He asked her to marry him on a glorious morning in late June. They had gone out together for a

ride, stopped in a very pretty glade, and dis-
mounted in order to drink from a crystal-clear
stream that ran rushing through the undergrowth.
Lord Rutherford tied the horses' reins to a tree
and bent down to scoop some water up in his
hands. "This is the best-tasting water in the
world," he said to Julie. "When I was a boy I
used to love to drink it." He looked hardly older
than a boy now as he knelt, slim and agile, over
the stream. His usually smooth brown hair was
ruffled and his brown eyes glowed with health
and happiness.

Julie followed his example and knelt to try the
water. As she bent over the stream he reached
out and touched the long blond braid that fell
almost to her waist. "Don't let your hair get
wet," he said, pulling gently.

The pressure on her hair brought back a disconcerting memory from the past. To banish it, she
turned to look at Lord Rutherford, assuring herself that it was indeed he and not someone else
who had touched her.

He looked back at her and his face was suddenly grave. "Miss Wells," he said. "Julianne.
My feelings cannot be unknown to you. Can you—
that is, do you—Oh, dash it all, Julianne, I'm
trying to say that I love you and I want you to
marry me. Will you?"

She looked up into the young and ardent face
above her. He was so sweet, she thought. She
smiled. "Yes, Lord Rutherford," she answered.
"I will be honored to marry you."

He smiled in return and moved closer to her.

"I'm so glad. I've been trying to get up the courage to ask you for days." He slid an arm around her waist. "You are so lovely," he said and kissed her.

Julie let her hand move up to lie gently on his shoulder. After a minute, and with obvious reluctance, he raised his head from hers. "When?" he murmured. "When will you marry me, Julianne?"

"That will be for Grandmama and your parents to say, my lord," she answered serenely.

"You must call me William."

"William," she repeated and he kissed her again.

This time it was Julie who halted the embrace, pulling back against his arm. It dropped immediately. "I think we ought to be returning to Minton," she said softly, and, with a sigh of regret, he agreed.

Lord Rutherford's announcement brought only happiness to his parents and the Dowager Duchess of Crewe. It seemed to be one of those fortuitous matches often dreamed about by fond parents and all too seldom seen realized. Both young people were well-born, good-looking, and wealthy. But more than that, they were so well suited in temperament and in interests that their future happiness seemed as secure as any earthly happiness can possibly expect to be.

Lord Minton was particularly pleased with the daughter his son proposed to give him. He saw in Julianne more than just a pretty face. He saw sweetness of temper and strong family affection.

Her dedication to her father during their years in Africa was particularly impressive. And Lord Minton was flattered by her obvious admiration of himself. The earl had three sons but no daughters and Julianne filled a gap in his family circle that he had not been aware existed until she came.

The visit to Minton lasted two weeks during which time Julie came to feel more and more comfortable and at home. Lord Rutherford had told her that his father would give them the family estate in Sussex to live in, but Julie said she would like to live at Minton, and the matter appeared to be settled. There was no more talk of Sussex and Julie looked forward to the day when she could truly call Minton her home. She was perfectly contented with the position of daughter; she felt no desire to be mistress of the house.

They were beautiful weeks, those weeks in June at Minton, before her engagement was officially announced to the world. Julie felt more content than she could ever remember feeling before. There was something so peaceful about Minton. The long vistas of lawn, the clipped trees, the tumbling fountains, and broad gravel walks were balm to her soul. She and Lord Rutherford would canter together in the leafy glades of the park, stroll up and down the paths in the garden, and feed the ducks in the ornamental lake. In the evenings she would sit over the chessboard with Lord Minton or look at albums of prints of paintings by old masters, and he would talk and she would listen attentively.

It was an idyllic time, tranquil and gardenlike in its freshness. Lord Rutherford was entranced by his promised bride. He had always thought her beautiful, and now, seeing her in his home, so gentle, so dignified, so feminine in her willingness to be instructed and guided, he fell more deeply in love than ever. When she allowed him to kiss her, and he felt her soft lips under his, it was very difficult to restrain his passion. He would look at her in the evening as she sat listening to his father, would look at her extraordinary, luminous eyes, her softly smiling mouth and lily-slender throat and feel himself impatient for his wedding day to arrive. It was set for November. He had not wanted to wait so long, but the Dowager Duchess had insisted and Julianne said they must abide by her grandmother's wishes. She was so sweetly compliant with the desires of those in authority over her. He looked forward to the day when she would have to be sweetly compliant to him.

The Fosters, of course, had no inkling of Julie's true character. They would not have recognized in her the girl who had shot a charging elephant, who had withstood the assault of her father's anger and disapproval for years, who had stood at a slave auction with regally frozen dignity, who had shouted at John Champernoun and then kissed him back with passionate abandon. It was not that Julie was deliberately trying to be deceptive about the kind of person she was. She thought she *was* being the person she was or, at any rate, the person she meant to be in the future. How was it possible to be anything but amiable and admiring in such surroundings, she asked herself. She would always be happy and secure and safe in such a place as this, surrounded by such people as these. This was the kind of life she wanted. She wanted to be like Lady Minton: good and peaceful and satisfied. Lord Rutherford would be the husband she wanted. Formed for domestic life and attached to country pleasures, he would give her all she desired out of life. She regarded as totally negligible the fact that she felt not a spark of passion for him. There were other things in life, she told herself, that were more important.

Chapter Eleven

Drawne was thy race, aright from princely
line . . .

—Sir Walter Ralegh

On April 9, 1815, the tenth Earl of Denham died
of pneumonia. The Earls of Denham had lived at
the family estate of Lansdowne in Kent ever since
the time of Edward III. They were among the
most aristocratic of England's nobles; the name
of Plantagenet appeared more than once on the
Champernoun family tree. But the fortunes of
the late earl had not been equal to his nobility.
Lansdowne was neglected and mortgaged; it
seemed that the new earl would be faced with
the painful task of selling one of the most ancient
family homes in the country.

The tenth earl had not been fortunate in his
progeny either. He had three daughters and no
sons. His younger brother had predeceased him,
killed three years earlier in a carriage accident.
He too had left only daughters. In consequence,

the title, the estate of Lansdowne, and the debts all devolved upon the late earl's first cousin, John, who had been out in Egypt for the last fifteen years.

Julie may have heard of the death of the Earl of Denham, but the news made no impression on her. Her grandmother was aware of the significance of the event, but did not trouble to enlighten Julianne. No one even knew if John Champernoun would come home. He had certainly never evinced much family feeling in the past.

The dowager duchess and her granddaughter returned to London at the end of June and the announcement of Julie's engagement was sent off to the newspapers. There was some collecting on bets in the clubs and the general feeling was that the dowager duchess had arranged a very advantageous marriage for her granddaughter. There was some gnashing of teeth among the matchmaking mamas who were not happy to have such a notable prize as Lord Rutherford taken off the market, but no one in the ton was really very surprised.

There was one person, however, not of the ton, who *was* surprised by the announcement he read in the *Morning Post:* "A marriage has been arranged between Miss Julianne Wells, granddaughter of the Dowager Duchess of Crewe, and William Foster, Viscount Rutherford." John Champernoun, now the Earl of Denham, stared at the words in astonishment. Then he slammed the paper down disgustedly on the table. For some reason he did not care to define to himself, the announcement had put him out of temper.

John had been in England for almost two weeks. When the lawyer had written to inform him of the death of his cousin, he had also communicated the unpleasant news that unless John could arrange for a miracle, Lansdowne would have to be sold. John did not care for Lansdowne, but neither did he want to be the one to sell the estate which had housed Champernouns for six long centuries. So, reluctantly, he had told the pasha he would have to return to England to straighten out family affairs.

He had put up at Grillon's Hotel, and for almost two weeks he and Mr. Stevens, the Denham family lawyer, had gone through the late earl's financial records. After all the debts had been verified, John had paid them. He paid off the mortgages on Lansdowne. He went to see his cousin's widow, who had returned to her father's home with her daughters and he arranged to settle some money on the girls. All in all, he appeared to the family and its devoted retainers to be an angel from heaven. He was the only Champernoun Mr. Stevens had ever known who had any money; and *this* Champernoun apparently had a great deal of it.

So far John had avoided returning to Lansdowne itself. It was a place where he had been deeply unhappy and he associated it with feelings of repression, anger, and hostility. He had been sitting over breakfast in his hotel room, pondering his next move, when the announcement of Julie's engagement caught his eye. It did not take him very long to decide it was time he paid a visit to his great-aunt, the Countess of Avanley. Lady Avanley was his grandfather's younger half-sister and the only person whom John remembered kindly from his childhood. She had paid periodic visits to Lansdowne and had always managed to bring a special treat to the orphaned little boy who was growing up there. When he had gone away to school it was she who would send him a few guineas for spending money. He supposed she was the closest thing to a mother he had ever had.

Lady Avanley had a house in Grosvenor Square. She had written him a note about a week before asking him to come and call on her, but somehow he had not yet managed to find the time to do so. He had not managed to find the time to see her when he had been in London last December either, but suddenly the hour seemed propitious. He called a hackney and in a very short time was being ushered into an elegant drawing room where he was greeted warmly by a stately-looking old lady.

"John! My dear, how lovely to see you." She stood on tiptoe to kiss his cheek. "Good heavens, how large you are!"

He smiled a little ruefully. "It's been a long time, Aunt Cecily."

"It most certainly has. Much too long. Sit down," she said firmly, "and tell me about yourself."

He sat down and regarded the straight-backed white-haired old lady whose blue eyes hadn't faded at all. "Well, I've been out in Egypt for the last fifteen years," he said easily. "When I heard George was dead and the estate about to be sold, I thought I'd better come home and see to things for a bit. I suppose you know Lansdowne was to be sold."

"Yes, I do know. And I know also that you have apparently become as rich as Croesus, something new in the annals of the Champernoun family. Mr. Stevens tells me you have ransomed Lansdowne and even settled money on those wretched girls."

He looked annoyed. "I thought lawyers were supposed to keep quiet about their clients' affairs."

"Mr. Stevens is perfectly trustworthy, my dear. However, he could hardly be expected not to inform me."

He sat back and stretched his long legs out in front of him. "You cross-examined the poor man," he said resignedly.

"Of course I did," she returned composedly. "You must have a glass of sherry with me, John." She rang the bell. "My husband has been dead for the last ten years," she informed her nephew with perfect and natural kindliness as they waited for the butler to answer.

He came in, the wine was served, the butler departed, and John was once again alone with his aunt. "I suppose I ought to have written to you," he began a little defensively. His Aunt Cecily's tactics while rarely direct were always effective.

"I'm sure you would have had you known," she replied serenely.

There was a little silence as she sipped her wine and he looked at her. Quite suddenly he grinned, his eyes blazing into brilliance. "All right, I give up. I apologize. I ought to have written. I ought to have come to see you sooner. Mea culpa. Will you forgive me or shall I leave?"

She met those eyes and her own softened. "I am pleased to hear you express such proper sentiments. I forgive you and you may stay and tell me what you plan to do with yourself for the next fifteen years."

He stayed with his aunt for another half an hour and when he left he had at least accounted for the next few weeks of his life. Lady Avanley was going to introduce him into the society to which he had always belonged by right of birth and in which he would hold some eminence by right of his newly acquired title and his undoubted wealth. He had managed to discover, by roundabout means, that the Dowager Duchess of Crewe was a friend of his Aunt Cecily and that he could expect to meet both the duchess and her granddaughter at the various affairs to which his aunt would sponsor him.

When John had been in London in December, he had made no attempt to broach the social scene. His mission had been purely political, and he had confined himself to meeting with the appropriate government ministers. He had been successful in his endeavors; at any rate, Britain showed no signs of moving against Mohammed Ali at present. But then, he told himself, there had been virtually no one in London in December. July was a different matter. It was the last month of the season and the ton were all gathered in the capital for their annual ritual of balls and receptions and dinners and love affairs and matchmaking. It might be amusing, he thought, to see what it was all about. It would be interesting to discover if anything about the English had changed during the years he had been away.

Chapter Twelve

He was a tall, handsome and bold man . . .
—John Aubrey

After the gardenlike atmosphere of Minton, Julie found London to be oppressive and irritating. Most girls would have relished their triumph in catching one of the ton's most eligible men, but Julie felt merely restless and bored. Lord Rutherford had returned to London as well, and he was diligent in his attendance upon his betrothed. It was not Lord Rutherford who was making her feel so dissatisfied, she told herself. He was as sweet, as good-natured, as agreeable as ever. It was the social whirl that was making her so edgy. There was no time, no space, no quiet. She longed to be back at Minton.

One afternoon she screwed her courage to the sticking point and took the manuscript of her revised journal to a publisher. She asked to see Mr. John Murray with a cool confidence she was far from feeling, and was secretly overwhelmed when she was ushered into his office. She had rarely felt more vulnerable in her life. The journal she was holding was like her child; it was part of her, more important than she would dare admit to a living soul. On her own she doubted she would have had the nerve to show it to a publisher. It was only her promise to John Champernoun that had brought her here on trembling legs.

Mr. Murray was very kind, very interested. She did not know that it was her fashionable clothing and her irreproachably respectable accompanying abigail which had got her in to see him. Young ladies who were clearly members of the quality did not often call at his office. Then, when he realized what he had got—the niece of the Duke of Crewe with a manuscript of her travels in Africa—his manner became even more approachable. He would be very pleased to look at her book. Would she call back in three days' time and he would tell her what he thought of it?

As soon as she left the office she had misgivings. Why had she allowed John to extract that promise from her? She was a fool to think she was a writer. Oh, they might very well publish her journal. It was a record of an interesting part of the globe. But she would expose herself in all her foolishness to the whole world. What would her grandmother say? What would Lord Minton think? She should not have done it.

The three days seemed interminable. She felt she would rather they turn it down than publish it just because of her name, of her father's name. She presented herself promptly on the morning of the third day and sat in front of Mr. Murray, her heart hammering in her chest.

The publisher looked soberly at the slender fair-haired young girl in front of him. "My dear Miss Wells," he said, "this is one of the most remarkable accounts I have ever read. I couldn't put it down. It's perfectly splendid." The young face opposite him began to glow. "I'll be honest and say I took it to read because of who you are. I never expected to find anything like this. You are both a naturalist and a writer, my dear."

She went home, fiercely happy. She had *done it.* She was a writer. She felt joyful and powerful and triumphant. She had not felt that way upon her engagement. She felt like shouting her news to the world.

It was when she reached home that some of her joy dimmed. Whom was she to tell? Whom could she share this triumph with? She knew enough about her grandmother to understand that she would not be pleased to see her granddaughter an authoress. She could tell William, of course. But he knew nothing of her life in Africa. He was rather a conventional young man; probably he would be a little bewildered by her desire to see herself in print. She wanted someone to exult with. And there was no one.

Her pleasure was dimmed by her silence. They were to attend a ball at Lady Heathford's that evening and she dressed for it automatically. Another ball. More of the same dull people saying the same dull things. She had to bury her excitement deep inside herself, to try to think of things that didn't really matter at all.

Lord Rutherford was waiting for her downstairs; he was to escort Julie and her grandmother to the ball. He smiled when he saw her, looking pure and regal in a new creamy satin gown. He bent to kiss her mouth and got instead a cool smooth cheek. He looked a little hurt. "Julianne," he said, then checked himself as the dowager duchess came into the room.

"Ah good, Rutherford, you're here. It's time we started." As they went out to the carriage the young man put a proprietary hand on Julie's arm.

They were late arriving at the ball. They were always late for social functions; the dowager duchess liked to avoid crowds at the door and on the stairs. The large ballroom was filled as they entered. Lord Rutherford bent to say something to Julie and she smiled and replied automatically. In the corner of the room, beyond his shoulder, she caught sight of a familiar figure, and she froze.

He was taller than anyone else; his head towered over the men who surrounded him. In that room of elegantly polished people he was instantly recognizable—clearer, brighter, lit with a more intense fire. For a minute Julie forgot to breathe and then his own gaze swung around and found her.

Lord Rutherford looked in surprise at the tall, dark man who was approaching his party with

such a purposeful air. He strode across the ballroom as if he owned it, unconscious of the watching eyes of the ton. He was the sort of man whom
other people would always watch.

It was the dowager duchess who greeted him.
"Good evening, Lord Denham. I am glad to see
you have come home."

Julianne's eyes widened. "Lord Denham?" she
asked in a startled voice.

"My cousin most inconsiderately died of pneumonia and I inherited the title," the black-haired
man said to her.

She chuckled with genuine amusement. "Are
you really an earl?"

Lord Rutherford was rather shocked at this
sign of levity in his betrothed, but Denham only
grinned. "I am."

"You deserve it," she said and at that the man
laughed.

"Lord Denham, you must allow me to introduce my granddaughter's fiancé, Lord Rutherford."

Those remarkable blue-green eyes were turned
on the young man. "How do you do, my lord," he
said a little stiffly. Lord Rutherford looked up to
meet that brilliant gaze and caught an expression
that startled him. It was gone in an instant and
Lord Denham was shaking hands, but Lord Rutherford was a little unnerved by the very unpleasant expression he had seen briefly in the other
man's eyes. Then Lord Denham was asking Julianne to dance and they went out together to the
ballroom floor.

"So that is the new Earl of Denham," Lord Rutherford said to the dowager duchess. "How does he know Julianne?"

"They met while she was in Africa," replied the old woman. "Lord Denham knew my son."

"I see," said Lord Rutherford tensely. He knew that John Champernoun had been out in Egypt. Lansdowne was not far from Minton and his family had naturally been interested in what was going to happen to the Denham family fortunes.

The dowager duchess looked at the young man's face and felt profound annoyance with the new Earl of Denham. Confound it all, she thought to herself, with healthy eighteenth-century vulgarity, why hadn't the man stayed in Egypt?

"Your fiancé," John was saying to Julie as they slowly circled the room. "You didn't waste any time, did you?"

His tone of voice was distinctly sarcastic, but Julie did not respond. She was too happy to see him. "Never mind Rutherford," she said impatiently. "John, you'll never believe what's happened. A publisher has taken my journal!"

His eyes blazed into the blueness she remembered so well. "I knew it!" he said. "Didn't I tell you? What did he say?"

"Mr. Murray said"—her voice bubbled with suppressed emotion—"that he couldn't put it down. He said parts of it were like poetry."

They were waltzing and now he pulled her closer to him and spun around in a breathless, twirling circle. Julie was laughing, her face raised to his. Her crown of golden hair came just to his mouth. "Everyone is looking at us!" she protested.

"Let them." But he slowed his steps. "I'm delighted. You have the eye of a born naturalist. And, as Mr. Murray said, you can write."

"I was so *glad* to see you tonight," she confessed. "I only found out this afternoon and I was *bursting* to tell someone. When I saw you standing there it seemed too good to be true."

"Ah," he said. "You haven't told Lord Rutherford?"

"No." For the first time since they had met she looked a little wary. "I'm not quite sure if he'll be pleased. They have such a feeling here about making oneself conspicuous. About *women* making themselves conspicuous, that is."

"Yes, well most women do not write like you do. Most women haven't had the opportunities to see the things that you have seen."

"Most women didn't have the father I had."

"True. You were very fortunate." There was no satire in his voice and she stared up at him, trying to see if he was serious. He was. "Do you think you would be a writer on the verge of having a book published if you had had a conventional upbringing?" he asked. "I decided long ago that my relations had done me a favor by driving me away. I've had a damn good time with my life as a result."

The music stopped, the dance was over, yet he made no attempt to return her to her fiancé. She scanned his face with searching gray eyes. He looked back at her, a curious lift to his straight black brows. She could not read what was in his eyes.

"Are you going to stay in England now that you've inherited?" she asked. "Or will you be going back to Egypt?"

"I don't know. I doubt if I could tolerate England on a permanent basis." He looked away from her face and across the floor. "Here comes your fiancé," he said blandly. "When is the date of your nuptials?"

"November."

"Ah, November." A faint smile curved his mouth as he watched Lord Rutherford come up to claim Julie. He was clearly a little ruffled by her behavior and John watched sardonically as she expertly set out to pacify him. The young man was obviously clay in her hands. After a minute she took him off to dance, leaving John on the edge of the crowd, his eyes following her proud golden head and slim white shoulders. Then Lord Castlereagh came up beside him and asked him a question. In a few minutes the two men retired to a private room and weren't seen for over an hour.

In the meantime Julie was having a perfectly wretched time. She danced with a great number of men, all of whom were extremely pleasant, and all of whom she found it difficult to talk to. After having had a *real* exchange with someone, it was hard to go back to mouthing polite, meaningless platitudes.

When John came back into the ballroom, the whole room came alive again. She watched as he talked with first one person and then another; watched how everyone watched him; watched as he danced with one or two women and watched their obvious attraction to him. He had tremendous power over people, she thought. Her father had had that quality as well. It did not stem from their remarkable good looks but from the strength of their personalities. They were both overwhelming and extremely forceful men—men whose mere presence made an impact on even the most grudging observer.

He was a dangerous man, John Champernoun. Dangerous to her. The surface veil of convention had been ripped away between them; they had shared too much with each other. She had told him things she would never tell anyone else. She had not seen him for eight months, yet she had felt more instantly at home with him than she felt with people who were far more intimately connected to her. They knew each other too well.

That was why he was dangerous. She had chosen her life and she was happy in that choice. She must not allow this intensely forceful man to come into that life and smash it. It was not as if she really *liked* him, she told herself. She could never like a man who was so like her father.

Chapter Thirteen

But all things are composed here
Like Nature, orderly and near. . . .
              —Andrew Marvell

The final month of the season came to a close at last and the ton prepared to desert London for the pleasures of the country. Julianne and the dowager duchess were to spend the month of August at Minton. The earl and countess had assembled a house party of friends and relatives who were anxious to meet the future Lady Rutherford—indeed, the future Lady Minton. In September the dowager duchess and her granddaughter would return home and in October there would be a house party at Crewe, hosted by the duke and duchess in honor of Lord Rutherford and his parents. In November the young people would finally be allowed to get married.

Julie was very glad to return to Minton. The tranquillity of the house would soothe away her restlessness. She was pleased also to see Lord

Minton again. He was everything she admired in a man: so good-humored, so intelligent, so utterly pleasant.

The Mintons had gathered a house party of some twenty people to meet Julianne and the dowager duchess. There were two of William's aunts with their husbands, three of his uncles with their wives and six cousins. The others were close friends of the family—Mr. and Mrs. Lewis and Lord and Lady Boldock. At first Julie had been disconcerted by the number of people; she had counted on Minton for tranquillity. But the house party was very easygoing and all the people so comfortable with each other that she was soon reassured. The atmosphere was as pleasant and serene as she remembered.

In the mornings the guests pretty much did as they pleased. Breakfast was set out in the breakfast room to be partaken of whenever one should happen to arise. Or one could breakfast in bed if one chose. The gentlemen usually spent the morning reading in the library or riding out on one of the earl's splendid horses. The ladies sketched or practiced their music. The afternoons were devoted to sports or the countess arranged an expedition such as a picnic or a visit to a local landmark. Dinner was served at seven o'clock, after which there was usually music and cards.

So passed the first week of August. Julie was making a conscious effort to devote herself to Lord Rutherford. He was so kind, so worthy, so steady, so *civilized.* She told herself a hundred times that she was lucky to have him. She would sit with him and ride with him and take a lively interest in all his doings and listen to his hunting stories for as long as he chose to tell them. In all this, she was so sweet and so good that everyone watching the young couple together was charmed by their obvious compatibility. It seemed to be a marriage made in heaven.

The second week of August began with a flutter of activity. Lady Minton announced that she planned to hold a ball in honor of the newly engaged couple. "I would like some of our neighbors to meet dear Julianne," she said, smiling graciously at her prospective daughter-in-law. There would also be a party for the tenantry, the servants, the local townspeople, and the yeomanry. Julie was a little startled by the magnitude of the celebration being organized.

"My mother and father have always held entertainments for the lower orders," Lord Rutherford proudly explained to Julie. "At my coming-of-age the festivities went on for three days."

"Heavens," said Julie faintly.

"My parents are always anxious to improve the relations between the classes. The Mintons have been Whigs for generations." There was the suspicion of a ring in his voice and Julie had to compress her lips a little to keep from smiling. The Mintons gave a party and thought themselves very liberal. She, however, was the daughter of a man who had done a great deal more for the "lower orders" than throwing an occasional entertainment. She had a large score chalked up against her father, but she had never questioned his sincerity. In the light of Lord Richard's commitment, the Mintons looked suddenly rather small.

As soon as she realized what she was thinking, she was horrified. How could she possibly ever criticize the way of life here at Minton? Hadn't she been wishing all month that a man like Lord Minton had been her father? She felt a pang of disloyalty at her critical amusement—disloyalty to her own chosen ideal of perfection. To make up for her brief defection she smiled up at her fiancé with warm admiration. "How splendid of them, William," she said softly.

"Julianne." His voice was not ringing now, but rough and a trifle breathless. They were alone in the rose garden and he pulled her into his arms and kissed her more passionately than he had ever done before. She let her hand lightly caress his smooth brown hair and idly noticed the beauty of the roses. When he raised his head he was breathing as though he had been running, a fact she remarked with clinical detachment. "I wish we hadn't got to wait until November," he said fiercely.

She smiled at him and gently patted his cheek. "I must do as Grandmama wishes, William. And I think she would wish that we go into the house now." She slipped a hand through his arm and began to walk him toward the open French doors.

"Yes," he said reluctantly. "I suppose she would."

*   *   *

Shortly after this disturbing incident during which her own thoughts had briefly turned traitor, Julie encountered another aspect of life at Minton that ruffled her determined admiration. The entire house party became infected by the acting sickness. It all started when George Foster, one of Lord Rutherford's cousins, proposed that they get up a play for the benefit of their neighbors. Apparently, amateur theatricals were very popular with the English upper class. Some of the great houses even had their own theaters, with a ballroom and a supper room attached. Minton was not so spectacularly equipped. The gallery would have to do as a makeshift playhouse, but Lord Minton promised that he would ask the estate carpenter to build them a stage.

It seemed that nearly everyone in the house party had acted at one time or another. It was decided that the play would be given twice, once for the servants and tenants of the Minton estate, and once for the quality of the neighborhood. After dinner one evening they all gathered in the library to choose a play and to assign parts. George Foster, who was twenty-three and enthusiastic, took charge. After a great deal of discussion, they narrowed the choice down to a comedy. In the end, it was George's choice that prevailed. They would do *She Stoops to Conquer*.

Julie had attended the meeting out of courtesy. It had never occurred to her that she would be asked to take part in this project, and she was appalled to hear William's cousin assigning her a role. "But I've never acted before!" she protested with alarm. "Surely you have a sufficient number of people without me!"

"Well, we don't," said George. "Not *young* ladies, at any rate. Don't fuss, Julianne. You'll be perfectly splendid. And you'll be playing opposite William." He smiled at her as if that must certainly take care of all her objections.

Julie cast a hunted look around the room. It was true what George had said about the age of the ladies. She and William's two cousins Anne and Maria were the only girls. And Maria had a stammer; Julie could understand why she would not wish to act. That left only Julie and Anne for the two heroines. Julie compressed her lips

She did not want to take part in this play. It all seemed very silly to her. She had no desire to display herself on stage for all the world to gawk at. It was not that she did not enjoy the theater. She had adored the plays she had seen in London. But they had been acted by *professionals*. She looked up to find Lord Rutherford watching her. "If you don't wish to act, certainly we will not force you," he said to her in a low voice.

"Could you not find a play that required only *one* young lady?" she asked him in the same tone.

"It has just taken us forty minutes to choose a play that had only two," he returned patiently. "Weren't you attending?"

She had not been. She looked around the room to find a sea of hopeful eyes watching her. She sighed. "Oh, very well. I suppose I can manage to get through it."

"You're a great gun, Julianne," said the enthusiastic George. "Wait till you see how much fun you will have!"

Julie doubted it, but she smiled pleasantly. "I'm sure you are right, George," she said and Lord Rutherford gave her hand an approving squeeze.

The disturbance she felt over the play, however, was as nothing compared to the alarm that ran through her at the announcement so calmly made by the earl a little later in the evening. "We have a new neighbor in residence," he said after he had accepted a cup of tea from his wife. He went to stand by the chimneypiece and everyone looked at him.

"Who is that, my lord?" asked Lady Minton placidly.

"Denham is at Lansdowne. The *new* Lord Denham, that is. I met him in town this morning and we had quite a pleasant conversation. Apparently, he found the property in sore need of repair."

"Well, the Denhams never had a groat to bless themselves with," said Frederick Foster, Lord Rutherford's brother. "I understand this new man is some sort of a nabob, though."

His father frowned disapprovingly. "There isn't a better blood line in the country than the Champernouns. Denham is certainly not a nabob. His father was the old earl's second son."

"But he is rich," put in Lord Rutherford.

"Yes." The earl nodded. "And I was very glad to ascertain that. It would be a shame to see an ancient family property like Lansdowne sold to some *real* nabob."

"It is so pleasant to have neighbors who are congenial to one," said Lady Minton serenely.

Julie had been standing like a frozen statue all during this conversation, but at Lady Minton's words she had a wild desire to laugh out loud. The thought of John Champernoun as congenial to the Mintons! She cleared her throat. "I hadn't realized that Lansdowne was in this neighborhood."

"Oh yes," said Frederick. "It is only a few miles to the east."

"I see," said Julie quietly.

Lord Minton looked at her curiously. "Are you acquainted with the family, my dear?"

"I met Lord Denham out in Egypt."

He smiled at her. "He is an extraordinary man, is he not?"

"Castlereagh is very interested in Denham," put in Lord Henry Melburne, one of the uncles who was in parliament and a member of the government. "He probably knows more about that part of the world than anyone else."

"Well, I invited him to come over to Minton for a few days. He seems a very pleasant fellow."

"And is he coming?" The voice was Lord Rutherford's.

"Yes, when he can get away from his estate agent, he said."

"Speaking of repairs, Uncle Minton," said

George, "do you think we might have a curtain with the stage?" And the conversation drifted off to the all-absorbing topic of the play.

It had been a nasty shock to Julie to hear that John Champernoun was living so close to Minton. It was even more alarming to discover that he was expected for a visit. For the next few days, and even though he had not yet arrived, his presence hung over her, looming and menacing. Every minute of the day she was braced to hear his name announced.

As if in reaction to her uneasy, turbulent mood, the weather changed. The cloudless skies of the first week of August turned dark and threatening and rain fell intermittently. The rain did not dampen the spirits of the house party members, who were plunged into rehearsing their parts for the play, but it made Julie even more restless.

She read through her part a few times, but even though the role of Kate was both witty and attractive, she could get up no enthusiasm for it. For the first time since she had been at Minton she began to feel confined, and late in the afternoon three days after Lord Minton had spoken about his invitation to the Earl of Denham, Julie decided to escape from the house and from all the eager thespians and go for a walk.

It was a dark and blowy day. The pleasant English garden did not suit her mood and she turned her steps eagerly toward the downs. It was lovely out on the hills. Julie had always been an inspired walker; she much preferred to walk than to ride on horseback, and she had had little opportunity to do more than stroll around gardens and shrubberies since she came home from Africa. She felt free and unrestricted out on the hill, with the wind whipping her hair loose from its stylish chignon, blowing her clothes and roaring in her ears. It was marvelous, she thought. She had not realized how cramped she was feeling until she had gotten out here.

It was with great reluctance that she finally turned back toward Minton. It was closing in on dinner time and she did not want to be late. She covered the ground quickly with her long effortless strides, but she had been away longer than she intended. There was a predinner party gathered in the drawing room as she came in by a side door and unfortunately Lord Rutherford was one of them. He saw her as she attempted to hurry past the open door unnoticed and called her name. "Julianne! I've been worried about you. Where have you been all afternoon?"

Reluctantly Julie paused in her flight and came to the door of the drawing room. Her hair had come down and she had pushed it back off her face by hooking it behind her ears. It hung, a windblown golden tangle, almost to her waist. There was brilliant color in her cheeks. She did not at all resemble the well-behaved young lady they were all accustomed to seeing. "I went out for a walk and stayed longer than I meant," she said to her fiancé. She looked quickly around the room in rueful apology and with a little shock of concussion met the brilliant blue-green gaze of John Champernoun.

Chapter Fourteen

————◆————

Who when retired here to Peace,
His warlike Studies could not cease. . . .
                            —Andrew Marvell

Julie changed her clothes with admirable haste, had her maid braid her hair into a coronet on top of her head, and was back downstairs by seven o'clock. Lady Minton, who had been resigned to pushing dinner back for at least half an hour, was astonished to see her. "You needn't have rushed so, my dear," she said gently. "We would have waited for you."

Julie smiled at her future mother-in-law. There was such peace, such kindness, in the eyes of Lady Minton. "I know, ma'am," she replied even more gently. "But *I* would have minded keeping you waiting."

They went into dinner and to her consternation Julie found herself placed between her fiancé and John Champernoun. "You looked as if you enjoyed your walk this afternoon," John said to her amiably as the soup was served.

"Yes, I did," she replied with less than amiable shortness.

"Feeling a bit 'cabined, cribbed, confined, bound in'?" he asked in mocking sympathy.

He had hit too close to a nerve for her comfort. She gave him a look that was wide and pure and cool as ice. "You are mistaken, my lord. I do not find Minton at all confining."

"I see," he responded equably. They had neither of them begun to eat their soup yet. He was watching her face and she was regarding her steaming plate with a noticeable lack of enthusiasm. She picked up her spoon and he said, twin sparks suddenly glowing in the depths of his eyes, "It must be that you are enjoying the prospect of acting. I understand you and Rutherford have the leading roles in this play you are doing."

Julie put down her spoon and looked at him. His expression was perfectly bland, but she saw the malicious sparkle in his imperfectly masked gaze. Her own eyes narrowed. "Don't bait me, John," she said, glancing at her fiancé and diplomatically lowering her voice. "I am content here at Minton. I am *not* going to allow you to rip up my peace, so stop trying. Do you understand me?"

"Yes." He was watching her still. "*Could* I rip up your peace?" His voice was low like hers, but unlike hers his was very soft.

She turned her head away from him and once more picked up her soup spoon. "No," she said calmly and definitely, "you could not."

He seemed to accept his dismissal, turned to

the table himself, and picked up his own spoon. Out of the corner of her eye she caught a glimpse of white on his hand and turned to look at it. He was holding the spoon a little awkwardly due to a bandage wrapped around his right palm. "What did you do to your hand?" she demanded.

"I cut it on a rusty nail in one of the sheds at Lansdowne. There is a depressing amount of rust everywhere on my ancestral estate."

"I hope you had it cleaned properly." There was an unmistakably sharp note in her voice. "Rust can be very dangerous."

The ghost of a satisfied smile touched his mouth. "I had it cleaned," he said.

For some reason Julie felt color coming into her cheeks. It was with great relief that she heard Lord Rutherford's voice addressing some remark to her. She turned to him instantly and for the remainder of the dinner managed to avoid any further extended conversation with her other dinner partner.

The food was superb, as it always was at Minton. The atmosphere also contributed greatly to a guest's enjoyment; the dining room was splendid, the table set with an impressive display of plate, and numerous footmen hovered, ready to see to any guest's needs. As the meal concluded, Lady Minton rose and ushered the ladies out of the dining room through the saloon and into the drawing room. The gentlemen remained behind to drink port, to smoke, and to talk.

When the men finally rejoined the ladies they

discovered that one of Lord Rutherford's aunts was playing the piano. Julie was seated on a small sofa by the window and Lord Rutherford went immediately to sit beside her. John, moving at a more leisurely but equally determined pace, sat himself down in a chair near both of them.

The music halted and Lord Rutherford looked at the black-haired man sitting at a right angle to him. The young man's handsome fresh-skinned face was a little more flushed than usual, his boyish mouth a little tighter. "Are you planning to make Lansdowne your permanent home, my lord?" he asked in a voice of careful courtesy.

"Well, that depends on what you mean by permanent," John drawled in reply. "When I'm in England I expect I'll stay there."

"You are not going to remain in England then?"

"I doubt it. I have too restless a nature, too great an interest in the rest of the world. England is so small."

Lord Rutherford stared at the strongly planed face of John Champernoun. Part of him was relieved to hear that Denham was not going to be his neighbor on a permanent basis; William was not completely easy about the obvious familiarity that existed between this man and Julianne. But part of him—the patriotic, nationalistic part—disapproved of an English lord becoming an expatriate. "Do you consider it right to give up your country?" he asked after a moment's pause.

"One can't give up one's country any more than one can give up one's grandmother," replied the other man easily. "They both preclude choice—

are elements of one's composition that cannot be eliminated."

"But you don't want to *live* in England?" The questioner now was Julianne.

He looked at her out of suddenly hooded eyes. "No. I don't. Not permanently. It's too narrow."

Lord Rutherford's warm brown eyes sparkled a little in indignation. "It is true that the Tories have controlled the government for years, but the time for a change is coming. The more liberal political elements will come into their own shortly, my lord. We, at least, do not intend to turn our backs on our country."

John did not look at all put out by this implied condemnation. "Are you a radical, Lord Rutherford?" he asked with interest.

"Yes, I am," replied that young man firmly. "My family have always been liberal Whigs, even from the earliest times."

"Ah well," said John blandly, "you've made a great success of it. I don't wonder you like it." And his sapient blue eyes traveled around the beautiful and elegant room in which they were sitting.

Julie's straight thin-boned nose quivered a little. Fortunately for her composure they were interrupted by George Foster, who pulled a chair up to the other side of the sofa. "Where were you walking today, Julianne?" he asked her curiously. "It was filthy weather. You really oughtn't to go too far from the house; there's no place to shelter from the rain."

John laughed. "Mr. Foster," he said, "I doubt if a little rain would bother Julianne Wells."

Julie looked annoyed, but it wasn't clear if her displeasure was directed at John or at George. "No, it wouldn't," she said evenly. "After being cooped up in the house for two days I felt the need to get outdoors, that is all. I went out to the downs."

"To the downs!" Both William and George stared at her, appalled.

"Do you know, Julie, it really would be kinder of you to disabuse these two young men of their image of you as a frail flower of English womanhood." John sounded distinctly amused. "The truth will shortly be revealed at any rate, won't it?"

He was referring to her journal. Julie thought for a minute, then looked into the worried, puzzled brown eyes of her fiancé. "Lord Denham is right, William," she said to him gently. "You seem to forget that I spent five years walking through the jungles of Africa. After that, a walk on the downs is child's play."

"But you had your father to protect you in Africa," Lord Rutherford said.

In reality it had been *she* who had looked after Lord Richard, but she did not say that to her fiancé. She smiled at him gently. "I am a tough campaigner, William. I learned to live off the country, to eat native foods, to sleep on the ground. My father maintained strict marching discipline; we walked regularly five or six hours a day no matter how hot it was or how rainy. The only thing that ever stopped us was fever. So you see, you mustn't worry about me. I am well able to take care of myself."

Lord Rutherford was staring at the pure and classically beautiful face of his future wife. He found it hard to reconcile what she was saying with the sweet, gentle, and yielding girl he knew. "Well," he muttered, "I don't like to criticize your father, but I think it was wrong of him to take you to Africa. I mean to take very good care of you in the future, Julianne." He smiled at her reassuringly, pleased at the thought of his future role. "I promise you, you won't ever have to sleep on the ground again!"

Very, very briefly Julie's eyes met those of John Champernoun.

Chapter Fifteen

> They know not I knew thee,
> Who knew thee too well ...
>
> —Byron

Julie did not sleep well that night and consequently arose later than she usually did. When she went down to the breakfast room she met Lady Minton, who informed her that all of the men who were not in the play had gone out riding. Everyone else, it seemed, planned to spend the morning rehearsing.

Julie stifled a sigh and drank an extra cup of coffee. Everything for the play was now in a regular train. The costumes had been decided upon and were being made by two local seamstresses. A scene painter had arrived from town and was getting to work in the gallery under the direction of George Foster. Most of the actors and actresses had learned their lines for the first three acts, and George was anxious to start rehearsing the individual scenes.

The sky was overcast but there was no rain as yet, so Julie slipped out to the garden with her copy of *She Stoops to Conquer* and sat on a bench holding it in her lap. She had been there for fifteen minutes before Lord Rutherford discovered her. He too had his copy of the play, but there was a preoccupied look on his face that told her his part was not what was on his mind.

Julie got up when she saw him. She felt a desire, for the moment, that he should not sit down beside her. "Were you wishing to rehearse with me, William?" she asked him pleasantly.

"I suppose we ought to." His brown eyes looked troubled. "George wants to run through the first three acts after dinner this evening."

She nodded. "Perhaps we should go inside, then. It looks as if it might rain at any moment."

He didn't move. "I've been thinking," he said. "What did Denham mean last night, Julianne, when he said that the truth about you would shortly be revealed?"

"Oh, that." She looked down at the playbook in her hands and turned it over. "I suppose I had better tell you. Mr. John Murray is going to publish the journal I kept while I was traveling in Africa."

"A journal?" he said blankly.

"Yes. Papa and I traveled to parts of Africa where no European has ever been, William. I kept a record of what I saw. It is rather a disorganized record, I'm afraid—comments on the habits of the elephant, the price of ivory, the customs of the natives, that sort of thing. But Mr. Murray found it interesting and desired to publish it."

"When did all this happen?"

"Just before we left London. I have not even told Grandmama yet. I haven't quite taken it in myself."

"But you told Denham." There was just the faintest trace of bitterness in his well-bred voice and Julie remarked it immediately. It made her uneasy.

"Yes. It was at his urging, William, that I set about publishing the journal, so naturally I knew he would be interested. I told him that night at the Heathfords' ball."

"I see." He turned to her with somber eyes. "For just how long have you known Denham, Julianne?"

Her sense of uneasiness increased as she looked up into his unusually grave face. "He was a friend of Papa's," she lied calmly. "It was Papa who showed him my journal." Her own gaze was wide, limpid, and pure.

Lord Rutherford looked deeply into those luminous gray eyes and slowly nodded. Julie had a sudden sense that she was safe, that even if he were not totally satisfied by her reply, his own great good manners would prevent him from questioning her further. She was right in trusting to his good manners, for in a moment he smiled and said, without a trace of the bitterness that had discomposed her, "Shall we go rehearse?" She followed him into the house feeling enormously grateful for his impeccable courtesy.

*   *   *

They rehearsed their first two scenes together, and on the surface all went well. Lord Rutherford was playing the role of Charles Marlow, an attractive, likable, but immature young man whose discomfort in the presence of "well-bred young ladies" was the springboard for the play's romantic comedy. Julianne was playing Kate Hardcastle, the well-bred young lady whom Marlow's father wishes him to marry. Their first scene was almost a burlesque, with Marlow so terrified of his prospective bride that he never once looks at her. It was a scene that completely reversed the usual role of courtship, with the man shy and tongue-tied and the woman assured and in charge, directing the whole course of the dialogue. Lord Rutherford's own physical attractiveness and natural modesty made him a perfect Marlow and Julianne thought she managed Kate's witty assurance decently.

Their second scene was a little more difficult for her. The basic premise of the plot was that while Marlow was inept and petrified in the presence of "ladies," he had no difficulties at all with "females of another class." In their second scene he meets Kate when she is dressed in simple country clothes and he takes her for a maid. It is a scene of high comedy in which Marlow, feeling superior and dominant and masculine, gets up a flirtation with the maid, while Kate, who thinks his mistake is hilarious, mercilessly leads him on.

Julie found herself feeling deeply uneasy as they rehearsed this scene. It was extremely funny and Lord Rutherford was excellent, but she felt herself to be stiff and uncomfortable. She apologized to him several times, but he was encouraging and would not admit that she was anything but splendid. She would have them all in a blaze of admiration this evening, he told her.

Julie slipped out by herself for a walk before tea. She went along one of the paths in the home woods, not intending to stray too far from the house. She had felt restless and dissatisfied all day and thought some exercise would help. It was drizzling and the feel of the light rain on her face, the softness of the dirt path beneath her feet, the silence of the woods were all deeply soothing. She strode along, covering ground with a steady gait, and tried to get a sense of perspective about her own feelings. *Why* did she dislike this play so much?

The answer to that question came to her as she walked through the cool, wet woods. She was feeling guilty. That was the cause of her uneasiness, her antipathy to the role of Kate. In Kate she saw too much of herself. Was not she deceiving Lord Rutherford just as mercilessly as Kate had deceived Marlow? Was not she just as manipulative? She had lied to William, and she intended to go on lying to him. She had taken advantage of his good nature. She was not just playing a role in this stupid play; she was playing a role in real life as well. Yet she could not tell him the truth about how she had met John. She could not tell him the truth about the slave auction. The very thought of his reaction to such a tale made her shiver.

She had gone further along the path than she had intended and she turned back toward Minton a little reluctantly. She recognized that reluctance in herself and it upset her. What was wrong with her, she asked herself angrily. How could she possibly be feeling this way? Was not Minton all she wanted out of life? Was not Lord Minton everything she had longed for during her years in Africa? Was not William the finest, most truly amiable young man she had ever known? The answer to all those questions was a resounding yes. She wondered a little bleakly, as she ran up the stairs to change her dress, why then was she not more happy?

The rehearsal that evening went with admirable smoothness. The stars of the show were undoubtedly George Foster, who was playing Kate's stepbrother, Tony Lumpkin, and William's aunt by marriage, Mrs. Henry Foster, who was playing Mrs. Hardcastle, Tony's mother. The two roles called for broad comic talent and the actors threw themselves into their parts with a combination of caricature and timing that made them truly funny. Anne Foster and William's cousin Francis were playing Constance and Hastings, the second pair of young lovers, and they acquitted themselves honorably, as did Lord Boldock and Mr. Lewis, who were playing the two fathers. Lord Rutherford made a boyishly charming Marlow and Julie remembered all her lines, which she felt was the best they could hope for from her. George, who was in charge as well as playing the role of Tony, was pleased with his cast. The onlookers, who comprised the members of the house party who were not acting, voiced their enthusiastic approval.

John Champernoun had been among the audience and Julie had been uncomfortably aware of his presence the whole time she had been on the stage. The play was a harmless diversion, she scolded herself, and everyone was obviously having a grand time. She ought to get over this feeling of discomfort. But it did not help to feel so intensely John's eyes on her as she recited Kate's witty lines. That blue gaze only helped to reinforce her conviction that she was being quite colossally silly.

The rain had stopped in the early evening and Lady Minton had the French doors that led out to the terrace opened. After she finished her tea Julie detached herself from the group of young people she had been sitting with. "I'm just going out to the terrace for a moment," she murmured in Lord Rutherford's ear.

She had risen and he made to follow her, but with her hand on his shoulder she gently pressed him back into his seat. "You stay and finish your tea." She smiled at him. "I just want a breath of the night air."

If she had wanted his company he would have joined her without hesitation, but now he watched her for a minute as she crossed the room and then turned back to the conversation he had been having with his cousin Francis. The two young men were soon happily absorbed in discussing the merits of a new horse that William hoped to hunt in the fall.

Julie stepped out onto the terrace and walked halfway to the stone parapet before she saw that she was not alone. She stopped dead for a minute, then took, at a slower pace, the last few steps that brought her abreast of the man who already stood there. The moonlight showed her his profile clearly. He waited a minute in silence before he turned to look down at her, one of his straight black brows lifted in irony. "Well, if it isn't Kate Hardcastle herself," he said suavely.

Julie compressed her lips. "Don't call me that."

"Why not?" He leaned against the parapet and regarded her inscrutably. "What should I call you, then? Shajaret ed Dur?"

Her eyes opened wide with shock at his words. She felt a thread of panic shiver down her spine. "No one knows anything about that, John. I thought we had agreed to keep it a secret."

"Even from your fiancé?" His voice was low and drawling.

"Yes. Even from him." She took an uneven breath. "I told him you were a friend of my father's. I told him it was Papa who showed you my journal."

He watched her without a flicker of expression in his strangely light eyes, then he put his finger under her chin and tipped her face up so it was illuminated by the moonlight. "Do you realize what you are doing by marrying this boy?" he asked her gravely.

She looked back at him a little uncertainly. There was no trace of mockery on his face. "Certainly I realize what I am doing," she answered, a small puzzled line puckering her clear brow. "What do you mean?"

"I mean," he returned grimly, "that you are not marrying Rutherford at all. You are marrying his house and his father."

She jerked away as if he had struck her. "That's not true!" She put her hands on the stone parapet and stared out into the moonlit garden. She was rigid with anger. "William is the nicest boy I have ever known. I am marrying him, not his possessions."

"Oh, I acquit you of being mercenary. That wasn't what I meant, and you know it. But I want you to think of this, my girl." He sounded almost brutal now. "On your wedding night that 'nice boy' whom you have been leading about like a tame dog on a leash is not going to be satisfied with a pat on the cheek. Have you thought about that? It's not his house you'll be going to bed with."

At that she whirled and swung her open palm at his cheek, hard and in deadly earnest. She was quick, but his reflexes were like lightning. He caught her wrist and held it in an unbreakable grip close to his face. They stared at each other in roused hostility and Julie felt the impact of his anger like a blow. Why can't we leave each other alone? she thought in a wild flash of despair.

There was the sound of voices approaching the French doors from the drawing room and the cruel grasp on her wrist relaxed. When Lord Minton and Lord Henry Melburne came out onto the terrace they found Lord Denham leaning casually against the parapet with Julie standing a good six feet away.

She felt a great rush of relief at the sight of Lord Minton. Here was safety, she thought. She gravitated immediately to his side and he smiled at her with that radiance of friendliness and good humor that had always so attracted her. He spoke a few words to John and the three men fell into general conversation, with Julie making no attempt to participate. She stood beside Lord Minton and watched John, and compared.

Between the Earl of Denham and her future father-in-law there appeared to be perfect respect and accord. But Julie thought that there could not be two men who were more opposed. Lord Minton represented peace and kindness and deep security. There was such a world of hereditary quiet in his blue-gray eyes, in the tones of his even, cultured voice. There was no quiet in John. He was energy—energy that was almost an irresistible power in itself. Like her father, he embodied strength and courage, adventurousness and ruthless determination. There was no peace in John's blazing eyes; the intensity of life was what burned there so clearly, so seductively.

But Julie had lived with a man like that. She knew how that ruthless energy could deprive her of all her freedom. She knew what it was to be haunted by the disapproval of such a man. Such a man had no respect for another person's selfhood, another person's separate interests and desires.

He attracted her. She was honest enough to admit that to herself. But she had been burned once, and badly. Never again, she vowed, stepping even closer to Lord Minton. She would take her nice, honorable, well-mannered William and count herself lucky.

Chapter Sixteen

━━━◆━━━

Gentle as falcon or hawk of the tower.
                                    —John Skelton

The sun was shining brightly the next day and Lady Minton announced that she had arranged an outing for the afternoon to see a beautiful fifteenth-century church in a nearby market town. They would take along a picnic and stop in a lovely spot she knew of for some alfresco refreshment.

The idea was greeted with enthusiasm by the young people of the house party, who by now were feeling the effects of the four-day rain. In the end it was decided to take two carriages and three phaetons. In the first carriage rode Lord Minton, his sister Lady Henry Melburne, and Lady Melburne's son Henry and daughter Maria. In the second carriage were Mr. and Mrs. Lewis and two Foster cousins. Mr. Frederick Foster drove his father's phaeton accompanied by his cousin George; Lord Rutherford drove Julianne, and Anne Foster had managed to maneuver so that she was riding with Lord Denham in his own phaeton.

They stopped for their picnic on the way to visit the church. Lord Minton supervised the unpacking of the refreshments while the rest of the party wandered about looking at the exceptionally pretty views they had of the channel in the distance. Lord Rutherford had Julie's hand tucked firmly in his arm and she was looking up at him with a trusting, almost childlike gaze. It made the blood stir in his veins, the way she turned to him like that, and his hand tightened possessively on hers.

"Rutherford." It was John Champernoun's voice. "I believe you said earlier that you wished to look more closely at my horses."

"Yes." For once Lord Rutherford was not anxious to have his attention diverted to horseflesh, but courtesy turned his steps toward Denham's phaeton. Julie was forced to accompany him. They were standing all three of them near the horses' flanks when there came a shrill scream from over by the trees. They turned as one. There, standing a few feet from the protection of the trees, was the most enormous dog Julie had ever seen. He was crouched, snarling at Maria, who was cowering some ten feet in front of him. The dog was coiled, ready to spring. The most frightening thing was not the growls that came from its throat but the white foam that flecked its muzzle and drooled from its mouth.

"Oh my God," breathed William softly.

"Don't move, Miss Foster." The voice was John's—cool, not loud but distinctly authoritative. He himself was moving, four steps back to his phaeton, where he reached a hand in quickly. He was back by their sides in an instant, a gun in his bandaged hand. "Julie," he said, and handed it to her.

"Denham!" The shocked voice was Lord Rutherford's, but Julie paid no attention as she raised the gun. Maria, panic-stricken, turned to run and the dog sprang. There was the sharp, loud crack of a gunshot and the dog crashed to the ground and lay still. John and Julie were the only ones to move for a minute, both of them walking swiftly toward the fallen animal. John looked down at the still form and said, "Good shooting. You got him through the brain."

Julie nodded. "Don't touch him. He was mad."

Their movement seemed to release all the others from the spell of shock. Maria turned, sobbing, into her mother's arms. Several of the ladies felt faint and sat down abruptly. A few of the gentlemen were pale as well. Lord Rutherford stared at his fiancée, who was handing the gun back to Lord Denham. Her face looked completely calm and fearless and as she glanced up at the tall man beside her a flash of something he could only describe as gaiety went across her lovely features. He was too far away to hear what she said and moved purposefully across the grass toward the two of them.

"You *would* have a gun handy," was what Julie had said.

"Of course I had a gun," he replied. "A reprobate like myself never stirs without one."

Lord Rutherford came to a halt beside them and looked with hostility at John's laughing face and brilliant eyes. "Good God, Denham," he exploded, "why did you give that damn gun to Julianne?"

John turned to him, black brows lifted in surprise. "My own hand is bandaged. I thought perhaps it might affect my accuracy."

"What I meant was, why did you not give the gun to *me*?" Lord Rutherford's face was flushed with agitation. Julie found herself thinking that he looked rather like a small boy who has been deprived of a treat.

"I know how well Julie shoots, but I didn't know about you," returned John bluntly. "It was not a moment for taking chances."

Lord Rutherford looked absolutely affronted. "John did not mean to insult you, William," Julie said reasonably. "I *do* shoot well, you see. And everything has come out all right. Except we really should bury this dog."

"Unfortunately, I don't travel with a shovel," said John regretfully and Julie laughed.

The sound of that rippling, genuine amusement infuriated Lord Rutherford. The two of them were behaving very badly, he thought. Neither showed the smallest concern for the feelings of others.

At that moment Lord Minton came up to them. "Good shot, Denham," he said.

"It was not Lord Denham who shot the dog, sir," came the stiff voice of Lord Rutherford.

"Oh? I thought, since it was his gun . . ." Lord Minton suddenly smiled. "Of course, you have hurt your hand. Well, believe me we are most grateful that you were along, Denham, and had the presence of mind to get that gun quickly to William. I shudder to think what would have happened if that dog had actually bitten poor Maria."

"William did not shoot the dog," said Julie with a trace of exasperation. "I did."

There was a moment of silence. "You did, my dear?" said Lord Minton.

"Yes." Julie was further exasperated by the undoubted incredulity she had heard in his voice. "I spent five years in Africa, Lord Minton. I learned how to shoot."

"I see." He turned to John. "It *was* your gun, Denham?"

"Yes. I have a pocket in the phaeton where I keep it. Like Julie, I spent too many years in Africa to feel comfortable if I don't have a gun at hand."

"Well, it was fortunate for us all that you had it," repeated Lord Minton.

The ladies now began clamoring to return home and Lord Minton turned to try to soothe and reorganize his party. In the end one of the servants who had come with the picnic was left to keep watch over the dog until a few men from Minton could arrive with shovels to bury it. The rest of the party hastily got into their carriages and in ten minutes they were on their way home, the fifteenth-century church quite forgotten.

Lord Rutherford sulked the whole way home. It was a well-bred, quiet sulk, but a sulk nonetheless. Julie kept her own temper under control and refrained from telling him exactly how childishly she thought he was behaving. When they arrived at Minton they found Lady Minton, the dowager duchess, and two Foster aunts in the drawing room, and the whole tale had to be told. Maria was bundled off to bed and the rest of the party settled down to tea and cake. They had been deprived of their earlier refreshment due to the dog.

It soon became clear that everyone was under the misapprehension that Lord Denham had fired the shot. No one had been looking at him; everyone's eyes had been fixed on the dog. They had seen Julie hand him the gun and assumed he had given it to her to hold while he examined the dog.

There was great wonder expressed when it became known that Julianne had fired the shot. John went through his explanation about his injured hand and everyone nodded doubtfully. They clearly still could not understand how he had ever given up his gun to a woman. Julie suddenly knew, with a flash of insight, that there was not another man in the room who would have done as John had. With the evidence of her marksman-ship staring them in the face, they still would not have given her the gun.

"But *how* did you know Julianne could shoot, Lord Denham?" asked Anne Foster sweetly.

"I knew Julie and her father in Africa," he answered easily. "I know how good she is with a gun. Lord Richard put her in charge of the firearms, in fact. I believe he found her to be more careful than himself about such matters."

Every eye in the room swung to Julianne. "Guns are very important when one is traveling in Africa," she explained patiently. "Aside from defense, they are one's chief source of food."

"Did *you* shoot the game for your meals, Julianne?" The incredulous questioner was George Foster.

"Most of the time," she replied evenly. "I was a better shot than Papa."

There was utter silence and then the dowager duchess said, "Dear Julianne finds it painful to talk about that awful time in Africa. Go upstairs to your room, my love. You need to rest after all this excitement."

Julie sighed. "It was not an awful time, Grand-mama. Some of it was wonderful."

"I know, dear," said the dowager duchess soothingly. "But I think you ought to go upstairs now."

Julie's lips curved in tolerant disdain as she looked around the room full of wide-eyed Fosters. "Very well, Grandmama," she said to the perturbed dowager duchess. "I will go upstairs." As soon as she had gone her grandmother began to explain and apologize for her unorthodox upbringing. Everyone was very kind.

Chapter Seventeen

Thus, by these subtle trains,
Do several passions invade the mind,
And strike our reason blind:
Of which usurping rank some have thought love.
　　　　　　　　　　　　—Ben Jonson

Several hours later Julie was seated before her dressing table getting ready for dinner. Her dress, a pale green summer gown of the lightest muslin, was laid out on the bed ready to be slipped on. Her maid was brushing her long hair preparatory to dressing it high on the back of her head *à la Grecque,* and Julie's eyes were closed. She loved to have her hair brushed; it seemed to her the absolute height of luxury to have someone else do this for her. Suddenly there was the sound of voices in the hall. Julie jumped to her feet, startling her maid into dropping the hairbrush. She picked it up, staring in bewilderment as her mistress walked swiftly to the door and opened it.

"I thought I heard your voice," said Julie with

satisfaction. "Come in here, I want to look at that hand of yours."

The very tall, broad-shouldered figure of Lord Denham appeared in the doorway. The maid's eyes widened in alarm as she perceived he was indeed coming into the bedroom. "It's a damn good thing for you George just went into his room," he said, looking at Julie's dressing gown and loose hair.

"Never mind about that. I want to see your hand," she repeated.

"It is all right, Julie."

"Get me a scissors, Nancy," she said to her maid, ignoring his words.

"Here, miss." The maid gave Julie scissors and stared with disapproval at John Champernoun.

Julie took his hand in a firm competent grasp. "Thank you. Now you may go get me some more bandage," she ordered calmly over her shoulder.

The maid's mouth opened. "And leave you *alone*, Miss Julianne?" she squeaked.

John looked at her sardonically. "If you hurry I won't have time to do anything too violently passionate before you return," he said.

Julie flashed him a brief repressive look as the maid scurried out, then turned her full attention to his hand. The bandage came off and she looked carefully at the healing wound in the palm. "Does that hurt?" she asked, pressing gently around the injured area.

"No."

She nodded with satisfaction and looked up at

him. "It seems to be healing well. There's no sign of infection."

His eyes were partially veiled by his lowered lashes as he looked back at her. "It was the bulk of the bandage I thought might affect my accuracy today, not any discomfort."

She was suddenly aware of him in a way she had not been before due to her preoccupation with his injury. She bent her head and looked again at the hand which she was holding. It was long-fingered, beautiful, and hard as iron. "One can't be too careful with puncture wounds," she said a trifle breathlessly. "I have a salve which I'll put on it for you."

He let her move away to rummage in a drawer, but when she turned it was to find he had followed her. He put his uninjured hand up and lightly touched her hair. It slipped through his fingers like heavy silk. "This was the first thing I noticed about you that day at the auction," he said, his hand buried now in the shining honey-gold length of it.

The conversation had taken a very dangerous turn and Julie knew she ought to put a halt to it immediately. She looked up into his eyes and felt as if she could drown in the sea-blue of them. "What else did you notice about me?" she whispered, very unwisely.

"Your skin." His voice was very soft, very dangerous. His hand had left her hair and was now on her jaw, moving caressingly down the line of it. Julie stood perfectly still under his touch, her face turned up to him, the salve held, forgotten, in one partially raised hand. "It is like touching satin," he murmured and his hand continued to move on down her throat. It slipped easily under the silk of her robe and came to rest on the bare curve of her breast. He left it there— light, undemanding, a gesture of absolute possession. She stared up at him with dilated eyes, her instinct being, as always with him, to yield. The tip of her tongue showed for an instant between her lips and his eyes darkened. In an instant she would be in his arms. Then the door opened.

"Here are the bandages, Miss Julianne," said the maid and John removed his hand.

"Thank you, Nancy," said Julie after a minute in a suspiciously husky voice. "Bring them here."

She bent her head, hiding behind the screen of her hair, and applied salve to John's hand. She wanted to kiss it and the desire frightened her. Her hands were not quite steady as they wound the bandage around his palm, but then, she noticed, neither was his. When she was finished she stepped back and looked at the cleft in his chin. She wanted to kiss that too. "That should do for a while," she said with determined steadiness.

There was a long interval of silence and finally she was forced to look up into his eyes. They were narrow and intent, and Julie was suddenly frightened by what she saw there, by what she knew she herself had provoked. "I will see you shortly, at dinner," she forced herself to say.

"Yes." His mouth was taut, angry-looking. "I will see you later."

The gentlemen lingered for an unusually long time over their port that evening and when they joined the ladies in the drawing room they were still in animated conversation. The chief participants were John, Lord Minton, and Lord Henry Melburne. They were talking about Egypt. Julie was immediately joined by Lord Rutherford, who was feeling a little guilty about his bad temper of the afternoon. He exerted himself to please and to charm her. He was an extremely nice young man and could be very charming indeed. Unfortunately, Julie was more interested in the conversation going on by the fireplace and his efforts were wasted. She smiled at him absently, but her attention was elsewhere. She could *just* hear what the men were talking about.

"You sound as if you admire Mohammed Ali, Denham," Lord Minton was saying. "But isn't he rather a barbarian?"

"It depends on what you mean by a barbarian," John replied evenly. "The fellahin of Egypt would infinitely prefer to be ruled by a barbarian like the pasha than by that mob of greedy bastard Mamelukes. I won't say the pasha is an enlightened ruler. The number of bad characters he has dispensed with without benefit of trial is enormous. But most of them badly needed dispensing with. And he has given stability to the government—something Egypt has lacked for centuries."

"He is not likely to be overthrown, then?" asked Sir Henry.

John quirked a black brow. "The pasha has a very effective way of dealing with any threats to his power. When he first took charge there were reports of discontent in the Arab quarter of Cairo. In response, Mohammed Ali promulgated a decree that anyone proved to have spoken disloyally of the government would be hanged on the spot. The next day I rode by the Ezbekiah Gardens and there were forty corpses hanging in rows by the roadside. There was a sign there also announcing that the victims had all spoken evil of the government."

"That was quick work. How did he have so many agitators discovered, convicted, and punished so swiftly?" The questioner was Lord Minton.

John's eyes gleamed with amusement. "Very simple. The pasha sent word to the chief of police that he must hang forty persons by daybreak. His orders were to pick out two score of the biggest scoundrels he could think of in the slums of Cairo."

"Good God!" Lord Minton looked appalled. "Then they were not guilty?"

John shrugged. "I daresay they had spoken, or would have spoken, disrespectfully of the government. At any rate, they were good riddance. And the pasha has had no more talk of popular discontent."

"He dealt quite as ruthlessly with the Mamelukes," said Lord Henry dryly.

"True. But then Egypt is not a civilized country," said John blandly. "It does not have Corn Laws, game laws, rotten boroughs, Acts of Suppression, and so forth."

Lord Henry, who was a member of Lord Liverpool's government, looked angry. Lord Minton, who was a Whig and did not approve of any of the measures just mentioned, looked scarcely less so. "All of those measures are most unfortunate, Lord Denham," he said a little stiffly. "However, there are those of us who are bound to try to change them. And certainly there can be no comparison between Britain, however troubled we may be at present, and Egypt. In England at least we are all free men."

"Ah, yes. Well, if we are going to discuss slavery we had better get Julie over here. *She* is the expert on that subject." John raised his voice a little and called her name.

Julie, who had been listening to every word he said, turned her head. "Yes?" she asked composedly.

"Lord Minton would like your opinion on slavery."

She smiled at William, took his hand in hers, and drew him over to the group of men by the fireplace. It was where she had wanted to be all evening.

Chapter Eighteen

Whoso list to hunt, I know where
is an hind ...
                    —Sir Thomas Wyatt

It was a stormy night and the weather matched the mood of at least three persons who retired to bed in the beautiful old house of Minton that evening. Lord Rutherford was feeling distinctly uneasy about the changes he had seen in Julianne since the coming of the Earl of Denham. His fiancée had always seemed to him the sweetest, gentlest, softest of girls. She had stirred his blood with her luminous beauty, her lovely, yielding disposition. She had made him feel both protective and possessive. He had thought he knew her quite well.

It was a conviction he was beginning to doubt. There was a core of ironlike independence and self-sufficiency in Julianne that he had never suspected existed. She had told him once that she was well able to take care of herself, and the

159

events of the day certainly seemed to prove that she had spoken the truth. She had made a shot that he could not have made. When all of the other women were trembling with fear she had been perfectly composed. And in conversation this evening she had spoken with authority about the brutality of the slave trade in Africa. He had been shocked by the things she had seen and experienced firsthand.

He had always known, of course, that Julianne had spent five years in Africa with her father. But he had never realized what those years had entailed. It had been impossible to imagine the beautiful fashionably dressed young lady he loved in any other setting than the one she now occupied.

It was impossible no longer. There had been something in her eyes tonight, and in her voice, that he had not seen before. And there had been an unspoken understanding between her and Denham that he resented and feared. It was as if they two inhabited the same world, as if their frame of reference, their system of values, their hierarchy of virtues, were unique to themselves. They were the initiated, and he, his father, and his uncle were not in their class.

Lord Rutherford was not regretting his engagement. Julianne was still the most beautiful and desirable girl he had ever known. He still wanted to make her his wife. It was Lord Denham he wished to see disappear from Minton. It was Denham, he decided, who was having this unfortunate effect on Julianne. He wished heartily that the man would go back to Egypt.

Julie was wishing the same thing. She felt completely turned upside down, completely upset. Her life had been clearly laid out before her and she had been happy in her choice of a future. Then John had come back, and all her peace, all her security, was lost. She could not write or read. She had lost contact with the Mintons, with William. Nobody interested her anymore but this one man.

It terrified her, her reaction to him. It was almost elemental in its power, its feel of inevitability. But it could lead to nothing but heartache. He didn't touch her life anywhere, not anymore. There was no future with him. He wanted her, but he would not marry her. He had told her once that he would never marry, and she believed him. He prized his freedom too highly.

She must find the strength to stay away from him. It was the only conclusion she could come to. It had been a mistake to call him into her room this evening. She must take care never, under any circumstances, to be alone with him again. He had been prudent once before, when she had been under his protection, but he would be prudent no longer. She had seen that in his eyes this evening. She must guard against him. Because if he ever got near her again she would melt like butter in his hands. It was a humiliating admission to have to make, but it was true. If only, she thought, he would go back to Egypt.

* * *

John Champernoun stood by his bedroom window staring bleakly out into the darkness, and his thoughts too were on Egypt. He should be returning east; the pasha would be looking for him. His business here was settled.

He knew why he was staying and the knowledge was not pleasant to him. It was Julie who held him. In this moment of painful honesty, he recognized also that it was Julie who had drawn him back, not his cousin's death. That had been only an excuse. He had known that this afternoon, the moment he had touched her.

She haunted him. Part of her power did indeed lie in her beauty; the first time he had seen her she had reminded him of a princess out of a fairy tale. But it was more than that. He had known and desired beautiful women; some he had possessed and some he had not. But never had any woman obsessed him as Julie did.

She was, he thought, more like a queen than a fairy princess: proud, strong, sufficient unto herself. The relentless, dedicated example of her father, the stoic creed of her mother, the strength bred of a lonely, difficult childhood and of the years of solitary struggle in Africa against intimidation, danger, and death—all had bred a spirit that attracted him more fiercely than even her beauty. It was an attraction that had drawn him back to England and was keeping him here—the one place in the world where he had sworn he would never live.

What was he to do? He wanted her. He wanted

her with an extreme desire, a desire that would only be assuaged by an act of possession. If the maid had not come back this afternoon, he knew he would have taken her. He could not have stopped himself. Nor would she have tried to stop him either.

He attracted her almost as strongly as she did him—he knew that. He knew also that she would not give up Minton and marry him; she had deluded herself into thinking that Minton and all that it represented was what she wanted out of life. She saw so many things so clearly—the quality of her mind had been revealed in almost every line of her journal—but she could not see herself. If she insisted on marrying Rutherford she would find out the truth about her own nature too late.

She must be kept from marrying Lord Rutherford. What happened after that . . . Well, he would cross that bridge when he came to it.

Julie spent the following morning riding out with Lord Rutherford and she promised to devote the afternoon to rehearsing their scenes together. George was going to have the cast go through the final acts in the evening after dinner.

Julie felt quite clearheaded and determined in the bright morning sun. She did not love Lord Rutherford, that she admitted to herself quite coolly. But she was fond of him and once she was married to him and had had his children, that fondness would grow and strengthen. She would never feel for him what she felt for John Cham-

pernoun, she admitted that also. But what she
felt for John was dangerous and untrustworthy.
She could be content with William. She would
build a family with him, would be a good wife to
him. His wishes would be her wishes, his ways
her ways, his honor her honor, his home her
home. He loved her and she was grateful to him
for that. She would always be able to rely on
him. They would have a good marriage.

Julie was helped considerably in her campaign
to stay out of John's way by a message that came
to him at Minton in the early afternoon. His
aunt, Lady Avanley, had arrived at Lansdowne
unexpectedly. John was forced to thank the Mintons for their hospitality and leave for his own
home in order to entertain his aunt. Upon his
departure both Julie and Lord Rutherford heaved
sighs of relief.

The next few days passed with unexceptional
regularity. The play was going well. The preparations for the water party that Lady Minton was
giving for the benefit of her tenants and the local
tradesmen were going well. Lady Minton's pro-
gram called for the play to be given on Friday
evening for the enjoyment of their neighbors and
such friends as were staying at Minton. The following day, Saturday, would be the dinner and
ball in honor of Julianne and William. And the
day after that, Sunday, would be the water party.

As Friday drew nearer, George drove his cast
with increasing concentration. The scenery had
been painted, the costumes were ready, and the
actors all knew their lines, but he insisted on

rehearsals. Most of the cast did not mind at all; they enjoyed the excitement of it. Julie did not like it, but she went along with the rest of the party and showed herself agreeable to whatever George suggested.

A week before Lord Rutherford would never have questioned her behavior, but now he found himself wondering. He wondered what it was she was really thinking behind that impenetrable patience of hers. He wondered why, if she was really as happy as she appeared, there were two faint half circles of strain under her eyes. He was developing the uncomfortable conviction that he did not know Julianne at all.

No one else appeared to notice anything amiss with either Lord Rutherford or his fiancée. Lord Denham was felt to be a loss to their party, but Lady Minton announced that he and his aunt would be returning for the play and the succeeding festivities. She had said this at tea one afternoon, and William looked quickly at Julianne to gauge her reaction. But he could read nothing in her profile, nothing in the hands so prettily and steadily stirring her tea. In a minute she had turned to him with a smile and a new topic of conversation.

As it turned out, they saw John Champernoun before the play on Friday. He rode over Thursday morning and invited Lord and Lady Minton along with whoever else wished to come to Lansdowne for the afternoon—to meet his aunt and see the house and grounds. Lord Minton was interested in seeing the estate and in talking to

John about improvements; he had found his former neighbor's impecunious state very distressing. As his father assumed he would be of the same mind, Lord Rutherford found that he was expected to go as well. And Julianne was included as a matter of course. So it was on a lovely August afternoon that Lord and Lady Minton with their son and future daughter-in-law as well as the dowager duchess drove over to visit the ancient home of the Champernoun family, Lansdowne.

Chapter Nineteen

Some fowls there be that have so perfect sight,
Again the sun their eyes for to defend . . .
　　　　　　　　　—Sir Thomas Wyatt

Lansdowne was a castle with a moat. Unlike so many of the great houses of the English nobility, it had not been renovated in the eighteenth century. The "new" wing dated from the time of Charles II, when the Champernouns, who had been faithfully Royalist, had known a brief moment of prosperity. It was perhaps more beautiful for being so relatively untouched, although the interior was not notably comfortable.

The grounds, however, were beautiful. Whatever money the previous earl had been able to put his hands on he had put into the part of the estate that showed. There were miles upon miles of lovely walks which wandered in and out of magnificent old trees, informal gardens, a rose garden, a sunken garden, and a lake. The furniture in the house might be faded and sparse, the wall hangings crumbling, the rugs in decay, but the grounds belonging to the house had been kept up. John informed Lord Minton that he could not say the same thing about the farms, a fact of which Lord Minton was already well aware.

Lady Avanley took Lady Minton, Julie, and the dowager duchess in charge while Lord Minton and William went off for a while with their host. Julie found herself liking John's aunt very much. She was brisk and efficient and after a short tour of the gardens she took the two older women back into the house for tea. Julie was given permission to wander about by herself for a little, which she was very happy to do. After her life in Africa she had never thought she would desire to be alone again, but she was finding the constant crowd of people at Minton to be rather trying. On a few occasions she had managed to slip off by herself, but that was not as easy to do as one might have imagined. One had to do it on the quiet; one could not simply announce that one was going for a walk alone. It appeared that English people thought there was something disgraceful about a young girl who desired solitude. Girls in England apparently traveled only in packs.

Julie enjoyed her solitary walk very much. The old trees and walks, the lovely gardens—all exemplified to her mind the best of England. She was so absorbed in her surroundings that the pricks of uneasiness that had been disturbing her serenity of late quite faded. She sat down on the turf steps that led down to a beautiful rose garden and just feasted her eyes. There was no one to disturb her. No one with whom she must make polite conversation. She folded her arms around her knees. She was happy.

An hour later John had returned to the house with his two male guests, and still there was no sign of Julie. The dowager duchess was very perturbed, as were the Mintons. John said easily, "If I know Julie, she is out communing with the flora and fauna. She'll come back when the trance is broken." He wanted to serve the light meal that had been prepared for his guests, but Lord Rutherford refused to eat. He would go look for his fiancée, he announced.

As he walked purposefully off through the garden, Lady Avanley said to John in a low voice, "You don't seem very concerned. After all, she *is* alone."

There was a distinctly saturnine look on his face. "I know. Poor girl, she gets precious few opportunities."

Half an hour later Julie and Lord Rutherford returned. She was full of apologies for losing track of time. "But what were you doing, Julianne?" her grandmother asked crossly. "You have made Lady Avanley put back her meal and worried all of us half to death."

"I was looking at the gardens," Julie said simply. "There was no reason for everyone to be worried. And you should not have waited for me to eat."

"Not *every*one was worried," put in Lord Rutherford evenly. "Lord Denham desired us to eat, but of course I could not think of such a thing."

Julie's reaction was not what he had hoped for.

"Good heavens, William, what on earth could have happened to me?" She looked distinctly annoyed. "You should have done as Lord Denham suggested and eaten."

William's lips tightened. For the first time since he had known him, John saw the young man angry. "There are all sorts of unsavory characters hanging about since the end of the war," he snapped. "Demobilized soldiers and sailors who have nothing to do but get into mischief."

"Are they the same 'poor wretches' you and your radical friends are so anxious to assist?" she asked with deadly sweetness.

"Well, we are glad to see you safely returned, Miss Wells," put in Lady Avanley briskly and tactfully. "And I can assure you, Lord Rutherford, that there are no unsavory characters wandering about the Lansdowne gardens. Now, if we might go into the dining room?"

As he walked past her to take in the dowager duchess, John murmured for Julie's ear alone, "I pity the poor unsavory character who runs into you."

She had to bite her lip to keep from laughing.

Lord Rutherford was extremely annoyed with his fiancée. He did not like her penchant for wandering off alone. And to look at the gardens! They were simply gardens, not unlike the gardens at Minton. He did not understand her.

She tried to explain. "It is simply that I love nature, William. It comes from spending so many years in Africa, I suppose. Among humans there was so much ugliness, with the slave trade and all, I mean, and nature provided an escape. It's—it's like my religion, you understand."

"No, I do not understand." He was sounding very annoyed now. "I can perfectly understand your appreciating the beauties of nature; that is something every civilized person must do. What I cannot understand is how you could disappear for two and a half hours and not realize that we would be worried about you. Two and a half hours! To look at a garden! By yourself!"

He could not understand and, given his background, it was not reasonable to expect that he should. Lord Rutherford was a member of the Whig aristocracy, perhaps the most relentlessly social society ever seen in England. Whigs liked politics, which for them consisted for the most part of personalities. They gave balls. They founded clubs. They played cards. They got up private theatricals. They had love affairs. They admired what was elegant and magnificent and easy to understand. Julianne was not easy to understand. When William spoke of it being "civilized" to enjoy the beauty of a garden, he did not mean the all-absorbing transcendence that she apparently felt. He meant "enjoy"—to look at it and see that it was pretty, and that was all. He was, to the very core of his being, a civilized man. From childhood he had been accustomed to move in a complex society, and the social arts were to him the essence of what civilization was all about. It was not civilized to spend two and a half solitary hours staring at a garden when you were a guest in someone else's home.

If he was blowing this incident all out of proportion, undoubtedly it was because it served as an excuse for him to voice the apprehensions he had been having all week about certain aspects of his fiancée's character.

Julie was perturbed by his reaction. She did not expect him to share her feelings, but she did expect him to make an effort to understand. The thought crossed her mind, and not for the first time, that though William was indeed very nice he was also utterly unimaginative.

They arrived back at Minton to be surrounded by a bustle of activity: The showing for the servants of *She Stoops to Conquer* was to be given in the evening. Julie tried valiantly to join in the general enthusiasm, but in her heart she was beginning to feel like some wild, caught creature in a vast and beautiful cage.

The performance for the servants went very well and the following day several more people arrived from London. The great house of Minton was bursting at the seams. Julie escaped with Lord Minton into the gardens for a part of the afternoon, but his company did not provide its usual delight for her. He had not changed; he was still the same good-humored, charming, intelligent man he had always been. It was just that as she looked into his quiet eyes she seemed to see beyond the deep security that had previously always been there for her; glimmering in their gray depths now was the faint reflection of a cage.

She returned to the house to find that John had sent her a copy of a poem. It was by William Wordsworth and was called "Lines Composed a Few Miles Above Tintern Abbey, on Revisiting the Banks of the Wye During a Tour, July 13, 1798." She went to her room and without even taking her hat off sat down to read it.

There were tears in her eyes when she finished. To think that someone could feel like this and could find such magnificent words to express those feelings. To find someone who *knew.* Her eyes went back to certain passages:

> . . . that serene and blessed mood,
> In which the affections gently lead us on,—
> Until, the breath of this corporeal frame
> And even the motion of our human blood
> Almost suspended, we are laid asleep
> In body, and become a living soul:
> While with an eye made quiet by the power
> Of harmony, and the deep power of joy,
> We see into the life of things.

"That is what it is like," Julie breathed, staring in wonder at the paper in her hand.

> . . . Therefore am I still
> A lover of the meadows and the woods,
> And mountains; and of all that we behold
> From this green earth; of all the mighty world
> Of eye and ear,—both what they half create,

And what perceive; well pleased to recognise
In nature and the language of the sense,
The anchor of my purest thoughts, the nurse,
The guide, the guardian of my heart, and soul
Of all my moral being.

It was what she had tried to explain to William
yesterday when she had said that nature was her
religion, and he had not understood.

The man who had sent her this poem understood. It seemed incredible, but it was true: Of
the two men—one civilized, educated, cultured;
the other an adventurer, a mercenary—it was the
latter who was the man of sensitivity and imagi-
nation. Under the circumstances it was not a
comfortable realization. But it was a realization
she could no longer avoid.

Chapter Twenty

And some, because the light doth them offend,
Do never peer but in the dark or night.
                              —Sir Thomas Wyatt

On the night of the play the great gallery at Minton was filled with eager spectators; the well-bred neighbors, friends, and relatives of the Foster family. One of the people packed into the rows of gilt chairs that lined the gallery floor was the Earl of Denham. He sat among the crush of upper-class strangers, his face inscrutable, his eyes on the closed curtain. His aunt, Lady Avanley, spoke to him once or twice and he replied pleasantly, but otherwise he made no attempt to socialize with anyone.

John had come to Minton for one reason only, and it was not to see the play. It was to see the girl who was taking the leading role. He did not have long to wait. The talk died away to an expectant silence, the curtains parted, and onstage was the main room of Hardcastle Hall, home of

Mr. and Mrs. Hardcastle. Mr. Lewis and Mrs. Henry Foster, who were representing that couple, began the opening dialogue.

It was five minutes before Julie made her entrance. She was dressed in an old-fashioned tight-waisted gown and her thick honey-blond hair fell in shining ringlets on her neck. John stared at the beautiful exposed line of her throat and heard hardly a word she was saying. He was startled when the audience laughed.

Julie was startled as well. They had laughed at this point last night also, she remembered, and it was a laugh that disturbed her. It came at the end of the following interchange of dialogue between Kate Hardcastle and her father:

MR. HARDCASTLE. Then, to be plain with you, Kate, I expect the young gentleman I have chosen to be your husband from town this very day. I have his father's letter, in which he informs me his son is set out, and that he intends to follow himself shortly thereafter.

KATE. Indeed! I wish I had known something of this before. Bless me, how shall I behave? It's a thousand to one I shan't like him; our meeting will be so formal, so like a thing of business, that I shall find no room for friendship or esteem.

MR. HARDCASTLE. Depend upon it, child, I never will control your choice, but Mr. Marlow, whom I have pitched upon, is the son of my old friend, Sir Charles Marlow, of whom you have heard me talk so often. The young gentleman has been bred a scholar, and is designed for an employment in the service of his country. I am told he is a man of excellent understanding.

KATE. Is he?

HARDCASTLE. Very generous.

KATE. I believe I shall like him.

HARDCASTLE. Young and brave.

KATE. I am sure I shall like him.

HARDCASTLE. And very handsome.

KATE. My dear Papa, say no more. (*kissing his hand*). He's mine, I'll have him!

Julie thought about the laughter that had greeted that last line as she stood in the wings waiting for her next cue. Lord Rutherford was on the stage with his cousin Francis, who was playing Hastings. She watched her fiancé's handsome face as she puzzled over her reaction and slowly the thought came to her that she had decided upon William in much the same fashion as Kate Hardcastle had said she would take the unknown Mr. Marlow. She, too, had had in her head a list of desirable husbandly virtues and when she had found a man who possessed them she had accepted him—without taking into consideration the man himself. It had seemed, at the time, to be a sensible thing to do. Now, with that laugh ringing in her ears, it seemed rather silly.

The play was a great success. George was glowing with pleasure as were, to a lesser degree, the other actors. Julie received her compliments with gracious modesty and went upstairs to change her clothes. A cold supper was to be served in the dining room.

At supper she sat between George Foster and Lord Boldock, but, although she conversed with them sensibly enough, her nerves were focused on the black-haired man who sat across the table from her. She never looked at him directly, but she was aware nonetheless of his smallest movement.

When the ladies returned to the drawing room, Julie found herself sitting next to Lady Avanley. "Your play this evening was delightful, Miss Wells," said the countess. "I quite laughed myself silly."

"I am happy you enjoyed it," replied Julie pleasantly. "Did Lord Denham like it also?"

"He certainly seemed to."

"I am glad," said Julie quietly.

"And *I* am glad to see him enjoying something as civilized as a play," said Lady Avanley. "He has been removed from civilization for too long."

"I would hardly call Egypt uncivilized, Lady Avanley." Julie's voice was very gentle. "There was a civilization on the Nile before England was ever heard of."

"You sound like my grandnephew," Lady Avanley said lightly. "He is forever castigating the insularity of the English."

"Perhaps," said Julie, even more gently than before, "he has a point."

"Perhaps." Lady Avanley looked at Julie with candid eyes. "I understand you knew my grandnephew out in Egypt, Miss Wells."

"A little. Lord Denham was a friend of my father's." Julie looked into Lady Avanley's shrewd gaze with eyes that were wide and clear and guileless. Unbidden, the memory of her father's comments on the "renegade Englishman" that was John came to her, and her nostrils quivered.

"You appear to have enjoyed Egypt." Lady Avanley's eyes had not missed that quiver. "Your father was a missionary, I believe?"

"Yes," said Julie.

Lady Avanley gave her a charming smile. "And now you have come home and are going to marry that nice Lord Rutherford. I wish you every happiness, my dear."

Julie stared at her hands, lying lightly clasped in her lap. "Thank you, Lady Avanley."

The countess sighed. "I hope John does the same, but I doubt he will."

"He can't marry Lord Rutherford," said Julie with amusement. "I believe there's a law or something."

Lady Avanley looked at her with arrested interest. "True," she murmured. "England is so parochial."

At that, Julie laughed. "What I meant, my dear,"

went on John's aunt, "was that I should like to see him settle down, marry and have a family. He is the last Champernoun and Lansdowne needs a son."

"Perhaps he will." Julie's voice was very low.

"I don't know." Lady Avanley sighed. "He came home at least. That is something. I thought he would let Lansdowne go, and one could hardly blame him if he had. He has no cause to love it, I fear."

"He did not get on with his uncle, did he?" Julie's eyes were on her hands so she did not see the assessing look Lady Avanley gave her.

"No, he did not. My nephew, the late Lord Denham, was a proud, cold, precise, and rigid man. He and John were complete opposites. It was most unfortunate that he should have been named John's guardian. He felt it was his responsibility to 'correct' John's personality." Julie's eyes flew to Lady Avanley's face and the older woman smiled a little at what she saw there. "Oh, I don't mean he beat him. George would never have done anything so crude. He used to lock John in his room. Often for a week at a time. Sometimes I used to think that it would have been infinitely kinder to have beaten him."

Julie knew all about punishments of isolation and silent disapproval. "Yes," she said in a muffled voice.

Lady Avanley shook her head. "Sometimes I've wondered if that early deprivation of freedom accounts for John's seemingly insatiable urge to roam the world. But I don't know if it does." She smiled ruefully. "Ever since childhood he has been a rebel. That's one of the reasons he rubbed against his uncle so. And nothing George could do to him would change him. He simply came out of his room and resumed his old ways."

"He is not a—safe—sort of a man," said Julie, staring once again at her hands.

"That he is not," his aunt laughingly agreed. "He is like the bad ice in a pond where one sticks up a danger sign. He has had a sign stuck upon him ever since he was a boy."

"Yes." There was the sound of men's voices in the saloon and Julie looked up to see the subject of their conversation coming into the room with Lord Boldock. He cast a swift glance around, saw her, and immediately started across the room. Lady Avanley sat back, a smile on her lips, and watched the slight rosiness that crept up into Julie's translucent cheeks. Lord Rutherford made an appearance right behind John, and Lady Avanley did not think that the look Julianne gave her betrothed was at all loving. It looked, in fact, distinctly impatient.

On the drive home Lady Avanley made several comments about what a handsome, well-suited couple the future Lord and Lady Rutherford would be. Her nephew, she was pleased to see, did not like them at all. Perhaps, John's aunt thought to herself as she got into bed, perhaps there was a chance of a son for Lansdowne after all. Then, as she snuggled down under the covers,

she remembered that tomorrow's festivities at
Minton were in honor of the betrothed couple.
Unhappily, it looked as if things had gone too far
to be recalled.

Chapter Twenty-One

> Others rejoice that see the fire so bright
> And wene to play in it as they do pretend
> And find the contrary of it that they intend.
> Alas, of that sort I may be by right . . .
> —Sir Thomas Wyatt

Julie's thoughts were running along lines that were similar to Lady Avanley's. She was beginning to realize that she had made a mistake, that she did not want to marry Lord Rutherford. But she did not see, either, how she was to get out of it.

Most of the gentlemen at Minton went out riding on Saturday morning and the ladies amused themselves by walking in the gardens or practicing their music. Lady Minton was busy with her preparations for the evening's dinner and ball, but she found the time to check on all her guests to see if they were agreeably occupied. Julie was sitting with her grandmother in the library and she watched Lady Minton's activities throughout the course of the morning. William's mother was extremely efficient and charming, with great dignity and style as she went from supervising the flower arrangements to looking in on her niece, who was playing the harp in the music room, to checking to see that the dowager duchess was properly supplied with paper and ink for her letter writing. Julie tried to imagine herself in Lady Minton's place, but somehow the picture would not come clear. Yet hadn't that been her highest ambition in life—to be like Lady Minton? Why did the prospect now seem so limited, so dull?

She went out driving with Lord Rutherford in the afternoon and the subject of her book came up. She had received a letter in the morning from Mr. Murray asking her if she wished her name to appear as the author.

"Of course you will not allow your name to appear in print," her fiancé said, clearly surprised that she should even consider such a possibility.

"But this is not a novel, William," she pointed out. "It is a book of true experience. How can I hide my identity?"

"If you insist upon publishing such a document," he replied stiffly, "you will subscribe yourself simply as 'a lady.' It is extremely improper for a woman's name to appear in print in such a fashion."

"But why? Everyone is sure to know who wrote it, anyway. What other 'lady' has traveled through Africa recently?"

"That is not the point. And if you had consulted me, I should have advised you against this whole venture. I don't understand how you came to do it in the first place."

She looked at his handsome boyish face. "Mr. Murray felt that the writing was extremely good," she said quietly.

"That's not the point," he repeated impatiently. "The point is that ladies do not publish without a sort of ... notoriety being attached to their name. I don't know what my mother and father will think. I haven't told them about this yet."

"I did not realize you felt like this," she said slowly.

He looked at her with a glimmer of hope in his brown eyes. "I can have the publication stopped if you wish."

She looked at him for a long silent minute and then shook her head. "I don't think so," she said gently.

His lips tightened. "I never knew you could be so stubborn."

She could get round him if she wanted—she knew that. She had only to touch his arm, to smile meltingly, to let him kiss her, to nestle very sweet and close to him, and he would let her have her way without further argument. She did none of those things. She drew a little away from him on the seat of the phaeton and said gravely, "Ah, William, I don't think you know me at all."

The dinner that evening was an ordeal for

Julianne. The state dining room was filled with people and more were due to come afterwards for the ball. The soft candlelight cast a lovely glow around the table; everything was beautiful, civilized, elegant, and polished. And all during the delicious impeccably-served dinner Julie was conscious only of a wild desire to be back in Africa: to be away from the people and the talk and the excessive food; to be eating a dinner of roasted impala on the white banks of a sand river, with nothing to listen to but the silence and the occasional sound of an animal. When Lord Minton stood up to toast the young betrothed couple, and Lord Rutherford took her hand in his, she heard in the glowing words of her future father-in-law the sound of a gate crashing closed behind her. She gazed gravely around the table and saw on face after face an identical look of smiling goodwill; her slowly moving eyes encountered a wrenchingly familiar blue-green blaze, and stopped. John's face was expressionless, but he had never been much good at disguising his eyes. She had seen in them anger and boredom, laughter and desire; at the moment they held an odd expression that it took her a moment to interpret. With a little shock she finally recognized it as pity.

Then Lord Minton sat down and William turned to her, and not long after that the whole party was in the ballroom. Julie led the first dance with Lord Rutherford, but what he said or how she responded she could not afterwards remember. The ballroom only became real when a very tall dark man came up to her and requested formally if he might have the next dance. Lord Minton handed her over with smiling good humor and went to talk to the dowager duchess. John and Julie moved onto the floor.

It was a waltz. The Mintons were very advanced people and did not disapprove of the new dance from Vienna. John held Julie lightly in his arms and silently regarded the shining honey-gold crown of her head. After they had circled the room twice she looked up at him. "I had a letter from Mr. Murray today," she said, seemingly at random. "He wants to know if he should put my name on my journal when it is published."

His straight black brows rose in surprise. "Whose name was he planning to put on it?"

"It seems it is not respectable for a woman's name to appear in print. William advises me to subscribe myself as 'a lady.' "

He swore and she laughingly protested, "John! You are in a ballroom, not a barracks."

His hand tightened over hers, hard and possessive. "You listen to me," he said grimly. "You wrote that book and by God your name is going to be on it. Rutherford hasn't read it. He doesn't realize what he is talking about. Damn it, Julie, that book is *good*. When everything is finally known about Africa, people are still going to be reading that book—to find out how it was, to find out how it all started. Someone is going to follow you up—you must know that. Someone is going to go back to look for that mountain, to look for those lakes—the source of the Nile." There was a note in his deep voice that brought a shadow to her face.

"You would love to be that 'someone,' wouldn't you?" she asked softly.

He smiled a little crookedly. "Yes."

He had to bend his head to hear her next words. "Will you go?"

His face was only inches from hers. He looked for a long silent moment at its proud beauty, then he said, with a very grim look about his mouth, "No. I won't be going." He swung her around a corner and continued after a minute, "You put your name to that book, do you hear?"

Her heightened color was not due to the exertions of the dance. "Yes, I hear."

He grinned. "And to hear is to obey?"

She frowned a little, then remembered the previous occasion on which she had used those words with him. She smiled demurely. "Well, not always. But in this case—yes. I will sign my name to the book. It's not as though I am ashamed of it."

"Ashamed!" He looked astonished. "Christ, Julie, that book is something to be proud of. And Rutherford should be proud of you for writing it. If I were he I'd shout it to the world."

The music stopped and they were forced to move off the floor, where they were immediately joined by George Foster. A little later in the evening John appeared again and asked her if she would care to step out onto the terrace with him. She accepted his invitation immediately but when they got outside they found Anne Foster and Henry Melburne. Both young people turned as

Julie and John came out the French door, and Anne said gaily, "Hullo there. Did you find the ballroom as stuffy as we did?"

John did not reply and Julie knew by the tightening of the muscles of his forearm under her hand that he was not pleased to discover company. "Yes," she said pleasantly in response to Anne's comment. "It was rather stuffy and Lord Denham kindly offered to escort me out to get some air."

"What about a brief stroll in the garden, Miss Wells?" John said quickly. "That ought to help clear your head."

"A good idea," Julie replied quietly.

"Yes, isn't it!" said the vivacious Anne. She had been angling for John ever since he had first come to Minton. "Why don't we do the same, Henry?"

"God damn it," muttered John to Julie as the four of them progressed down the terrace steps. "It was easier quelling the Wahabi uprising than it is to see you alone."

"Yes," said Julie sadly. "One does always seem to be surrounded by people here." And she smiled at Anne, who was standing waiting for them.

Julie did not get to bed until close to three o'clock, and even then she did not sleep. She lay awake, staring at the moonlight shining in her open window, and faced grimly the knowledge she had been successfully avoiding for so long. But she could repress it no longer. It was there: clear, whole, and inescapable. She loved John Champernoun. And that love was like a huge gulf that separated her from everything she had known these last few months. The face of everything was changed: Minton, William, the life she had thought she wanted. Nothing was, or would ever be, the same again.

She had thought she was safe. She had thought she could never love a man like her father—a restless rover, an adventurer, a man who would never be satisfied to sit by the fire and watch his children, to ride through his fields and watch the corn grow.

How had it happened? How had it happened that when John had said tonight "If I were he," her heart had leaped and she had thought wildly, If only you were. If only it were you I was going to marry.

She had been telling herself for weeks that it was only a physical attraction she felt for him, but she knew tonight that it was more than that. If he should ever ask her to marry him, she would say yes with a glad heart and go with him wherever he wanted to go. She had thought she wanted a home like Minton, but she knew now that no place would ever be home to her unless he was there.

How had she been so blind to her own feelings? How had she allowed herself to become engaged to Lord Rutherford?

The answer she thought, lying perfectly still beneath her sheet and blanket, lay with her father. She had been telling herself since she met John that he was just like Lord Richard. But he wasn't, not really. Her father had been a relentless man;

everything and everyone had to be subdued to his own inflexible mission. He had no respect for the individuality of others.

John was not like that. He was the only person she had ever met who was willing to let her be what she was, who was not anxious to force her into a mold of his own making. She had railed at him about his code of "personal freedom," but in fact it was what she loved in him. He was the most genuinely independent and free man she had ever known. He was the slave of no convention and he refused to enslave anyone else.

Given a chance, however, Lord Rutherford would. If she married him she would never write. She was deadly certain of this tonight, the night her engagement had been formally announced with such generous hospitality. If she married him she would become just like Lady Minton—very charming, very dignified, but not profoundly interesting or thoroughly impressive. She would—shrink.

And John? She closed her eyes and her lips compressed with pain. She would give her soul to marry John. But he would never tie himself down to a wife. She remembered Said's remarks about John's feelings in regard to women and babies. He would never allow himself to be bound by a family. He prized his freedom too highly for that.

But she loved him, and knowing that she could not marry Lord Rutherford. It would not be fair to him. It was a thousand pities she had not realized the truth of her feelings before this week-end of festivities. But it could not be helped. She would tell him tomorrow that she was breaking their engagement.

The dawn was lighting the sky before she finally fell asleep.

Chapter Twenty-Two

———————

For to withstand her look I am not able,
Yet can I not hide me in no dark place . . .
                                        —Sir Thomas Wyatt

The day of Lady Minton's water party dawned clear and bright. Guests from the Minton house party mingled with the estate tenants and tradespeople from the town. There were rowing boats available on the lake and the guests from the lower class could partake of refreshment in the large striped tent that had been set up on the lawn. A cold supper was to be served for the house party and friends in the dining room, and after dark there was to be a fireworks display.

Julie wore a summer dress of white lace slotted through with pale pink ribbon. A ribbon of the same color confined the soft knot of hair on the top of her head. She looked very young, very lovely, and very fragile. Lord Rutherford had smiled with pleasure when he saw her and Lord and Lady Minton both complimented the dowager duchess on her granddaughter's appearance. The Mintons were also very satisfied with Julianne's behavior. The modest and graceful self-possession with which she greeted a bewildering variety of tenants and tradespeople was very impressive.

Julie was feeling extremely uncomfortable. The morning had not brought with it any change of heart. She still could not marry Lord Rutherford, but the social consequences of her breaking their engagement were assuming enormous proportions. After this kind of a celebration, her begging off was going to prove a deep embarrassment to the Mintons. And Julie genuinely liked and respected them. She liked William as well; she just did not want to marry him. She was beginning to think, however, that she had better wait another week or so before she informed him of this disconcerting fact.

The afternoon progressed smoothly, with the lake filled with noisy, happy boaters and the tent filled with hungry, happy eaters. Other guests strolled about the gardens or sat in the shade of the splendid old trees. There was, however, no sign of the Earl of Denham or his aunt, and Julie was beginning to be afraid that they were not coming. She was not even sure if they had been invited, and once or twice she started to ask William but then thought better of it.

At one point late in the afternoon Julie caught her dress on a bush without realizing it and as she walked forward the lace tore. She had been walking with her grandmother and Lord Rutherford and all three stopped when they realized what had happened.

"Oh dear," said Julie contritely. "I'm so sorry, Grandmama. I'm afraid I've torn this lovely dress you gave to me."

"It does not seem to be too serious, my love," replied the dowager duchess. "If you return to the house my dresser will mend it for you in a trice."

"I'll go with you, Julianne," offered Lord Rutherford and she smiled absently at him and put her hand on his arm.

They were going in a side door of the house when they heard the unmistakable thuds and grunts of a fight. "Good heavens," said Julie in a startled voice, "what is happening?" Before Lord Rutherford could stop her she had stepped around some concealing hedges in pursuit of the sounds. Lord Rutherford was right behind her and they both saw at the same moment two furious young men, dressed in their Sunday best, apparently trying to kill each other with their bare fists. They were the sons of two of Lord Minton's tenants and Lord Rutherford recognized them immediately.

"Austin! Franklin!" he said in a peremptory, imperious tone. "Stop this instantly, do you hear me?"

But not even the clipped authoritative tones of the aristocracy penetrated the blood haze that had overtaken the two young men. They continued to pummel each other.

As Lord Rutherford hesitated, unsure of what to do next, there came another voice from behind him. "Here, we can't have this," said John briskly and he stepped into the middle of the fight. The intrusion of a third party seemed to inflame the first two even more and Julie watched with hammering heart as John became the target of the boys' frustrated anger.

It took about two minutes before one of the boys was down on the ground, dazedly holding his head, while the other was held motionless by a very efficient and painful grip on his arm. John's lip was bleeding, his shirt was torn, and he looked perfectly happy. "This is hardly the sort of behavior one expects to find at Lord Minton's garden party," he said regretfully. "I'm sorry for it, gentlemen, but the fight is over."

The boy on the ground shook his head and, as his vision cleared and he took in the sight of Julianne and Lord Rutherford, the eye that was not swollen shut widened. "My lord," he mumbled. "I didn't know . . ."

Julie glanced at William's angry face and quickly put a soothing hand on his arm. "Are you able to get up?" she asked the boy on the ground. Then, as he staggered trying to do so, she instructed her fiancé coolly, "Help him, William." Without a word Lord Rutherford went to put a steadying hand under his arm.

Julie turned her attention to the other boy, who was already on his feet and looking almost as horrified as his former adversary. "You had all better come into the house with me," she said calmly. "I'll clean you up and then, gentlemen"—she looked with strict gray eyes at the culprits—"you had better go home and cool off." She turned, bent to pick up John's discarded coat, and meekly the four men trailed after her into the house.

The two youngsters were clearly overwhelmed by the commotion they had caused. Julie took them into the morning parlor, washed the blood off their faces and hands, and efficiently applied salve and bandages. All the while she was doing this, John sat on the edge of a table, swinging one leg, watching her and holding a clean handkerchief against his lip to stop the bleeding.

Lord Rutherford tried to find out what it was that had caused the fight, but both boys were shamefaced and evasive. At last John said with amusement, "Leave them alone, Rutherford. It was a girl, obviously." At this both boys blushed a deep red and Julie had to bite her lip.

"Well, if that is so, then I am certain she would be ashamed of you both if she knew about this," she said severely. They hung their heads and Julie put her hand up to her mouth and coughed. She couldn't look at John or her gravity would be completely overset. It was hard to reconcile these two meek and embarrassed lambs with the furious and belligerent fighters of twenty minutes ago.

"Rutherford," said John smoothly, "perhaps you would see these two on their way? I don't think we ought to trust them in each other's company for too long a time."

"Why don't you take them?" asked Lord Rutherford with a noticeable lack of his usual courtesy.

John removed his handkerchief. "My lip is still bleeding," he said regretfully. With tight mouth and angry eyes, Lord Rutherford herded his tenants out of the Minton morning parlor and toward the side door they had come in a short time before.

There was silence in the morning parlor after they left. Then Julie looked at John. "You enjoyed that!" she said accusingly.

He patted his lip with the handkerchief one last time. "I like a good, dirty fight." He grinned a little crookedly, favoring his cut lip. "Alone at last," he said.

"I shouldn't count on that," she replied after a minute, striving to keep her voice normal.

"True." He looked at her and there was no trace of amusement at all in his face. "You are driving me insane, do you know that?"

"I haven't meant to," she replied honestly.

"I know you haven't." His voice sounded bitter. He stood up and came over to tower in front of her. What he would have done next she never knew for at that moment there was the sound of her grandmother's voice in the doorway.

"Julianne! Whatever has happened? Rutherford told me you were in need of my assistance."

John had only time to mutter, "Meet me after supper by the boathouse," before the dowager duchess was upon them.

Chapter Twenty-Three

Remembrance so followeth me of that face
So that with teary eyen swollen and unstable
My destiny to behold her doth me lead;
Yet do I know I run into the glede.
                            —Sir Thomas Wyatt

The dowager duchess dismissed John and took Julie upstairs to have her dress attended to. Then it was time to repair to the dining room for supper and Julie sat next to Lord Minton and felt horribly guilty under the warm approval of his smiling gaze. She tried to make up to him for her treacherousness by being as admiring and responsive as she possibly could. She did not notice the very bleak look that crept into a pair of watching blue-green eyes.

It bothered John to watch Julie with Lord Minton more than it did to watch her with her fiancé. He had a pretty accurate estimate of what her feelings were for Rutherford, and he did not doubt that when the pinch came he could discount the boy as unimportant. Lord Minton was different. There could be no clear-cut rivalry between him and Lord Minton. In the earl Julie saw the father she had always longed for. John did not make the mistake of thinking her feelings were more complicated than they were. Nor did he do Lord Minton the injustice of thinking his affection for Julie was anything other than paternal. But that was precisely why he was so dangerous to John. He could fight and conquer a romantic attachment; it was this other love that he feared would bring about his defeat. He was beginning to think that drastic measures were called for in order to put an end to Julie's engagement.

He was out of temper when he met her down by the boathouse at eight o'clock. The dusk was creeping in and the boats out on the lake had lanterns hanging on their sides, reflecting their glow in the sheen of the water. John assisted Julie into a boat, lit their own lantern, and pushed off strongly with the wooden oars. He rowed for a few minutes in silence and then said savagely, "This bloody society. We have to sneak around like a pair of criminals in order to find fifteen minutes to talk to each other!"

"I am a lot freer here in England than I would be if I were living in Egypt, or any Arab country for that matter," Julie pointed out sensibly.

John swore in Arabic.

"I know the language," she said gently.

They were in the middle of the lake by now. All around them lanterns floated on the darkness of the water; the boats themselves were almost indistinguishable. He rested his hands on the oars, let the boat drift, and looked at her. "I'm sorry," he said.

She could just see him in the light of the lantern. His hair had fallen across his forehead almost to the straight black line of his brows. His lip was just slightly swollen. She wanted very much to reach out and touch him. "I love you," she said instead.

His head jerked up. "What did you say?"

"I said I love you," she repeated.

"Julie . . ." He leaned forward and took her hand in his. The lamplight fell on his hair; it was so black that there was no trace of brown in it at all. At that moment the entire lake exploded with light. The fireworks had begun.

Julie laughed a little tremulously. "There's a conspiracy," she said shakily.

"Yes." He had begun to row back toward the boathouse. She could see the muscles working in his arms and shoulders as the fireworks continued to illuminate the night. The boat moved swiftly and smoothly through the water. He was very strong.

Lord Rutherford was waiting for them at the boathouse with Anne Foster. "Goodness, Lord Denham, but you row well," said Anne while William cast a sharp eye on his fiancée's composed face.

John smiled absently and staggered a little as he got out of the boat. "I believe I must have gotten hit in the head in that little—encounter— this afternoon, Rutherford," he said. "I felt unaccountably dizzy out there on the water."

Lord Rutherford, who was quite genuinely kind, put an arm under John's. "Let me walk with you up to the house, Denham. Perhaps you should lie down for a bit."

John leaned on him. "Perhaps I should," he muttered and allowed Lord Rutherford to lead him off. Anne followed, begging to be allowed to help, and Julie stayed on the landing looking after them with narrowed, speculative eyes. She didn't believe for a minute that John had been dizzy.

Lord and Lady Minton believed him, however, and he was urged not to ride back to Lansdowne but to spend the night at Minton. He demurred at first but soon allowed himself to be persuaded. He went up to bed at ten o'clock. The rest of the house party retired at midnight and by one o'clock the house was silent. It was two o'clock, and Julie was still lying sleepless in bed when her door opened silently and John came into the room. She was not surprised to see him. She had known all along that he had had some ulterior motive for wishing to spend the night at Minton.

He closed the door behind him and came over to stand beside the bed. She was lying back on her pillows, her hair tied loosely at the nape of her neck with a blue ribbon. The moonlight streamed in the window Julie always insisted be left open to the sky. She didn't move but looked up at him steadily out of dark eyes. "How is your head?" she asked composedly.

His mouth quirked a little in reply. "Better." He sat down on the side of the bed and his shoulders blocked the moonlight. She didn't move, didn't say anything. "You have haunted me," he said softly to her quiet, watching face. "For almost a year now I have not been able to get you out of my mind. I thought when I left you here and went back to Egypt that I would be rid of you. But I wasn't." He reached out and gently pulled the ribbon that was tying her hair. He held it up, looking at its soft blueness in the moonlight.

"Why did you come here?" she whispered.

His shoulders, clad only in a soft white shirt, looked enormous as he bent toward her. "To make love to you," he said. "Do you want me to go away?"

Her eyes were wide and grave and dark with acceptance. "No," she said, and with that one single word burnt all her bridges.

She melted as soon as he touched her. Her arms went up around his neck and when his hand slipped under her nightdress to caress her bare skin she trembled and shut her eyes but she did not object.

John felt that tremor and tried desperately to put some brakes on his own passion. He did not want to frighten her, he did not want to hurt her. But at last he had her where he had wanted her for months and when she arched up against him, kissing him with innocent yet passionate abandon, his control broke.

Afterwards they lay in each other's arms, at peace. He reached out and smoothed a long strand of hair back from her cheek, then kissed her softly. "Did I hurt you?" he murmured.

He had, but it didn't matter. "No," said Julie. "You didn't hurt me." She closed her eyes and put her cheek against his shoulder and listened to the strong, steady beat of his heart.

"You won't marry Rutherford."

"No." Her voice was steady but it sounded strained.

He frowned a little. "You wouldn't be happy with him. You must know that now."

"Yes." Her face remained hidden against his chest.

"You said you loved *me*."

She raised her head. "Surely you aren't doubting that now?"

She was supporting herself on one elbow and looking down into his face. The guarded, wary look she saw in his eyes surprised her, but then they narrowed a little and quite another expression crept in. "Kiss me," he murmured. Slowly she lowered her head until her lips met his. His mouth was gentle and she felt herself relaxing. He put his arms around her and kissed her eyes, her nose. "God, but I love you," he muttered and then his mouth once again found hers. White fire flickered deep inside her as the soft sleepy mood of contentment receded to be replaced by the flaming rush of passion. The world receded as well and nothing was left but the delirious melting pleasure of John's touch, of his mouth. Blindly, eagerly, passionately, she followed where he led. Afterwards she went to sleep in his arms.

Chapter Twenty-Four

———◆———

Such art to greve, and after to make gladd,
Such fear in love, such love in majestye.
                    —Sir Walter Ralegh

Julie slept deeply and dreamlessly, making up at
last for all the restless nights she had spent of
late. When she awoke her room was flooded with
sunlight and John was gone. She felt utterly deso-
late without him. Slowly she got out of bed. She
was about to ring for her maid when she saw an
envelope propped up on her dressing table. It
said merely "Julie." With a curious reluctance
she picked it up, hesitated, and then opened it.
His strong, masculine handwriting leaped up at
her.

I am going to London for a short time.
That ought to give you a chance to break
your engagement to Rutherford. I'll come
to see you at your grandmother's.

Be patient, sweetheart. I am trying to work things out for us.

John

Julie read the letter through three times and then she tore it up into little pieces and threw it away. There was a curious, almost blind look in her eyes that her maid assumed was residual sleepiness. "I've brought you a nice cup of chocolate, Miss Wells," she said encouragingly. "You had a good, long sleep. It's almost ten o'clock."

"Is it?" said Julie, absently accepting the cup. Obediently she drank it and allowed Nancy to dress her in a morning frock of soft blue muslin. She went down the stairs rather like a sleepwalker, avoided the breakfast room, and went out into the garden. Her fiancé found her there fifteen minutes later.

"Would you like to go for a drive with me, Julianne?" he asked her.

She hesitated, then replied firmly, "Yes, William. I would. I want to talk to you."

They didn't say anything else until they were in his phaeton. Then he said briefly, "Let's go to the folly. We can be private there."

She nodded gratefully, leaned back, and tried not to think as the carriage was drawn briskly along the beautiful avenue of Minton. After a while William turned off to a side path that led them eventually to the small, almost comically Gothic structure that had been put up by Lord

Rutherford's grandfather. He helped Julie out of the phaeton and they walked together toward the sixty-year-old medieval ruin. They stopped under the shade of a huge beech tree and Julie said simply, "William, I cannot marry you."

There was a white line around his mouth. "I had an idea that you were going to say that. It's Denham, isn't it?"

Julie hesitated, looked at him, then said, "Yes."

He took her shoulders in his hands and stared down into her lovely troubled face. "I love you, Julianne." His voice sounded harsh.

She smiled a little. "No, William. You don't love me. You love the person you thought I was."

"I don't know what you mean."

She reached up and very tenderly touched his cheek. "Yes, you do. You love the Julianne who held your tackle while you fished, who listened to your hunting stories, who let you show her how to drive and how to play cards. You don't love the Julianne who has to get away by herself sometimes because she is dying of suffocation from too many people. You don't love the independent, self-sufficient Julianne who took care of herself and her father for five years in Africa. You don't love the Julianne whose journal is going to be published by Mr. Murray."

"I don't mind your being independent," he said stiffly.

"Oh, William." She watched him steadily, her eyes narrowed with pity. "You would hate being married to a woman who is a better shot than you are."

"You are not a better shot!" he said quickly. Her only reply was the rueful smile that crept into her eyes. He exhaled an angry breath. "Are you a better shot than Denham?"

"I don't know. But, you see, if I were he I wouldn't be at all upset. He'd be proud of me."

"And I suppose he's proud of your book, too."

"Yes," she said very gently. "He is."

He had been holding her shoulders all through this conversation, but now he dropped his hands and began to pace around. "If you loved him why did you say you would marry me?" he asked accusingly, coming to a halt some four feet away from her.

"I mistook my own feelings," she replied quietly. "The blame is all mine. I thought I wanted the kind of life your mother and father have. And, then, William, I liked you so much. I still do like you enormously. But I cannot marry you. It would not be fair for me to do that. You don't want a wife who loves another man."

"You're right," he said tensely. "I don't."

She made a small, apologetic gesture. "I am so sorry. I ought never to have allowed your parents to go through with that lovely celebration. But I did not realize myself how I felt until just two days ago. At the ball, in fact. Now I will embarrass them, and you, and I have put them to such terrible expense."

Lord Rutherford sighed and showed his quality. "Don't worry about the money or the social embarrassment. I will take care of that."

"Thank you, William." She smiled at him, a

little tremulous with relief. "You are so utterly decent and good-natured and sweet. I feel like a wretch for putting you in this position."

A small muscle flickered next to his mouth. "A lot of good my virtues have done me." He sounded bitter. "When are you going to marry him?"

She bent her head, refusing to look at him for the first time since the interview had begun. "I don't know."

There was a pause. "Perhaps I ought to have said *are* you going to marry him?" He had come closer to her, his feet silent on the thick grass.

"Probably," she said.

"Probably? Has he asked you?"

"Not yet."

"I see." He turned her face up so he could look into her eyes. "Is he likely to ask you?"

Julie returned his look, and then, because he *was* so sweet and decent and because she felt in his debt, she told him the truth. "He will ask me to marry him, but I do not think he will stay with me. John is not a man for the joys of domesticity. He will probably settle me at Lansdowne and come back periodically to renew his acquaintance."

"I see. And you won't like that."

"No, I won't like that."

"Then perhaps I ought to ask if *you* are planning to marry him."

She smiled a little wryly. "I'm afraid, William, that I've come to the point where any crumb from the table will be better than nothing. Yes, I will marry him."

His face looked very bleak. "I don't at all like the idea of your being at Lansdowne. My head tells me you are right to cry off from our engagement, but the rest of me isn't so sure."

She exhaled a long, slow breath. "You will be. And I'm really not sure what John will do. I shall just have to wait and see."

"What does a girl like you see in a man like that?" He spoke with a mixture of bewilderment and anger. "I grant you he's good-looking in an uncivilized sort of way, but he's an adventurer—a man with no sense of patriotism or social responsibility."

It was not possible to explain to him what it was she saw in John, so instead she smiled. "I am an adventurer myself, William. I loved being out in Africa. I'd like nothing better than to trek off with John on a search for the source of the Nile."

"Good God! Certainly he wouldn't allow you to do that!"

"No, I don't think he would. He has a very poor opinion of the inconvenient habit women have of producing babies. That is just the sort of behavior that would slow up an expedition."

He stared at her for a minute in silence and then said tightly, "Shall we go back to the phaeton?"

She agreed and when they were once again trotting along the wide avenue he began to speak of some new ideas his father had for expanding the stables. She listened and replied, grateful to him for his chivalry and his courtesy. When they reached the house and he came around to the carriage to assist her down, she said only, "Thank you, William. You are indeed 'a verray parfit gentil knight.' "

He stood for a minute, his hands on her waist, looking up into her face. Then he swung her down. "Yes," he said and the note of bitterness was very audible. "I know."

Chapter Twenty-Five

When I was gonn shee sent her memory
More stronge than weare ten thousand shipps of
warr . . .

— Sir Walter Ralegh

Julie and the dowager duchess returned home to
Crewe two days after Julie's conversation with
Lord Rutherford. He had advised her to say noth-
ing to her grandmother until after they had left
Minton, just as he would say nothing to his
parents.

"It seems so cowardly of me," she said doubtfully when he proposed this course of action to
her.

"It may be cowardly, but it is far more considerate of others," he replied firmly. "It will pre-
cipitate an extremely awkward situation if we
announce our broken engagement while you are
still here. The social strain would be enormous."

Julie had bowed to his superior knowledge of
social propriety and had gone off with warm

farewells from the Mintons and promises to see her shortly. She felt utterly hypocritical, but it could not be helped.

Her grandmother had first been stunned, then incredulous, and finally furious when Julie had told her the truth. She too had said almost immediately, "It's Denham, I take it." Julie had not been aware that her partiality for John was so obvious. It didn't help her pride to realize that the whole world had apparently seen her wearing her heart on her sleeve.

And where was he? One week went by and then two, and still there was no word from him. Life at the Dower House was hardly pleasant. The dowager duchess barely spoke to her granddaughter and when she did it was only to make remarks such as, "You're a fool to throw away a man like Rutherford," or "You've thrown away one of the best positions in the country, do you know that?" The dowager duchess had little use for the Earl of Denham. "He hasn't even asked for you," was the comment that hurt Julie most. She was all too aware of that distressing fact.

It was a golden day in September when he finally came. Julie was cutting flowers in the garden when she looked up and saw him striding down the path toward her. For a moment her heart seemed to stop, and she knew, as she watched his oncoming figure, that never would she feel this way about anyone else. She met his eyes, so brilliant and blue in his dark face, and knew also that she would do whatever he wanted, and on his terms. She loved him so much.

He smiled at her but there was an odd, grave look in his eyes. "Your grandmother is not pleased with me. She just informed me that if I were going back to soldier in Egypt she would not allow you to come with me."

"What did you say?"

"I told her that I would not ask you to do such a thing." He looked at her reassuringly. "Why do you think I have been in London? I wrote you I would arrange things for us."

He was going to leave her at Lansdowne. In her deepest heart she had known that that was what he would do. He misinterpreted the look on her face and said, holding out his arms to her, "I put you in a position where you would feel you had to marry me. I know that, and I did it quite deliberately. But I don't mean to coerce you into a way of life that would not be suitable for you."

She went to him and buried her face in his shoulder, feeling the strength of his arms around her. "Do you mean you wanted me to marry you?" she asked, her voice muffled by his hard shoulder.

He put his cheek against her hair. "I have wanted nothing but you, almost since the first moment I saw you. It was only when I saw you with Rutherford, though, that I realized how deeply I felt. I knew then that I had to break that engagement, that it was I you were going to marry. It was the accomplishing of that plan that proved so difficult."

She was conscious of deep surprise as she listened to him. She moved her face away from his shoulder and looked up. "You said you would never marry."

His mouth twisted. "I shouldn't. I can't offer you the life you want. It wasn't Rutherford I was afraid of, you know. It was his father. And his home. You told me once you would never marry a man like me, a man incapable of settling down. And I just can't live the rest of my life at Lansdowne, Julie." He sounded a little desperate. "It will be our home, I promise you that. It will always be there for us to come back to. And we will spend a part of every year there, I promise you that as well. But I am not a Lord Minton. It would drive me wild to try to become like him."

Julie scarcely heard the last part of his speech. It was the "we" that she focused on immediately. It sounded as if he did not mean to leave her behind after all. "I knew that if I made love to you you wouldn't marry Rutherford," he was saying now. "It wasn't fair, perhaps, but then I couldn't afford to be fair. I couldn't afford to lose you."

She stared up into his vehemently masculine face, a face that was graven forever on her heart. "Oh, John." Her voice was low and shaky. "I would have married you in an instant. Minton lost all its attraction the day I saw you again. I don't care about settling down. I don't care about being safe. I only want to be with you."

"Is that true?"

"Yes."

They looked at each other for a long, silent

moment and then he said, quite softly, "We've both been fairly caught, haven't we, sweetheart?"

She nodded, mute under his gaze, and then he was kissing her eyelids, her mouth, her throat, her mouth again. After a minute they moved to one of the stone benches and continued what they were doing. It was Julie who finally pulled away. "There's no place we can go," she said huskily.

"Damn." He was trembling almost as much as she was. "We'll get a special license and be married next week."

"All right." Prudently, she moved a little away from him on the bench. "You haven't told me what arrangements you made in London."

He took a deep steadying breath and spoke almost normally. "I've been appointed special ambassador to the Sublime Porte."

He smiled at her look. "It's true. It looks as if the sultan is going to be at war in Serbia shortly. And he is trying, inefficiently I fear, to modernize his empire. There are a few things that Castlereagh wants me to find out for him."

Julie began to laugh.

"What's so funny?" he asked equably.

"Somehow you are not my idea of an ambassador," she said, looking at his lawless face.

He was unperturbed. "I was ambassador to the Porte for the pasha in 1810. I know the sultan and his advisers rather well." He grinned at her and held out an arm. "It's safe to come back now." When she had nestled in the crook of his

arm, he continued. "Turkey may be rather enjoyable. We can do a bit of traveling—across the
Aegean to Greece, across the Black Sea to Russia.
You should find plenty of material for another
book."

She closed her eyes for a minute. She was so
blissfully happy it hurt. "Are you planning on
making a career out of being a special ambassador?"

"Possibly. There are plenty of problem spots
in the world that could use my attention. It has
its attractions. It is even respectable, and if I am
to be a husband and a father I had better resign
myself to being respectable."

"We ought to learn some new languages. It would
be grand to see St. Petersburg and Moscow."

He laid his cheek for a minute against her hair.
"And South America."

She sat up, her eyes luminous. "South America!
Think of the birds, John!"

His eyes narrowed as they looked at her glowing face, but before he could reach for her again
Julie said, "Here comes Grandmama."

He turned to watch the martially erect old
lady coming toward them down the garden path.
"Do you think she'll approve of my making you
the wife of an ambassador?" he asked.

"I think so." She slipped her hand into his and
they both rose to their feet. "If she doesn't," said
Julianne with great sweetness, "we shall just
have to elope."

"I'm afraid you are an adventuress, Miss Wells,"

he murmured softly and she looked up at him and grinned.

"Yes," she said cheerfully, "I'm afraid you are quite right, my lord." And so, linked together, they stepped forward to greet the oncoming dowager duchess.

About the Author

Joan Wolf is a native of New York City who presently resides in Milford, Connecticut, with her husband and two young children. She taught high school English in New York for nine years and took up writing when she retired to rear a family. Her previous books—THE COUNTERFEIT MARRIAGE, A KIND OF HONOR, A LONDON SEASON, A DIFFI-CULT TRUCE, THE SCOTTISH LORD, MARGARITA, HIS LORDSHIP'S MISTRESS, and THE AMERICAN DUCHESS—are also available in Signet editions.

Other Regency Romances from SIGNET

SIGNET Regency Romances You'll Want to Read

Buy them at your local

bookstore or use coupon

on next page for ordering.

SIGNET Regency Romances You'll Enjoy